I0618454

Nothing But Time
A Family of Worth
Book One

Sherry Ewing

Kingsburg Press
San Francisco, California

OTHER BOOKS BY SHERRY EWING

Medieval & Time Travel Series

If My Heart Could See You

Hearts Across Time: The Knights of Berwyck,
A Quest Through Time Novel (Books One & Two)
A special box set of For All of Ever & Only For You

For All of Ever: The Knights of Berwyck,
A Quest Through Time Novel (Book One)

Only For You: The Knights of Berwyck,
A Quest Through Time Novel (Book Two)

A Knight To Call My Own

To Follow My Heart: The Knights of Berwyck,
A Quest Through Time Novel (Book Three)

Regency's

Under the Mistletoe
A Kiss for Charity
Nothing But Time: A Family of Worth, Book One

Find Sherry and her work at www.SherryEwing.com

Nothing But Time
A Family of Worth
Book One

Sherry Ewing

Kingsburg Press
P.O. Box 475146
San Francisco, California 94147
www.KingsburgPress.com

Front Cover Photo by SelfPubBookCovers.com/woofie_2015
Front cover fonts, Spine and Back Cover Design by Claudia Bost at www.designsbycwb.com

Editor: Jude Knight

Nothing But Time: A Family of Worth, Book One/Sherry Ewing -- 1st ed.
ISBN 13: 978-0-9971777-7-0
ISBN 10: 0-9971777-7-2
eBook ISBN: 978-0-9971777-8-7
Library of Congress Control Number: 2017905763

DEDICATION

For my dearest friend Stephanie.

You and I have been to hell and back over the years spanning our friendship. Through all the laughter and tears, I know you're always only a phone call away, although we really need to cross the bridge and have some face to face time soon. Thank you for always being there for me, along with your wonderful husband Paul who reads my books as your stand in.

I love you Steffie… to the moon and back!

ACKNOWLEDGMENTS

A special shout out and word of thanks to my beta readers, Jude Knight, Tricia Linden and Caroline Warfield for taking time out of their busy schedules to read *Nothing But Time*. You ladies went above and beyond in your comments to make my work better, and I appreciate all your efforts.

I would also like to thank Jude Knight for her editing services. You took my final document and made it shine. Thank you for helping me find the holes in my plot or solving questions regarding this period in time. I couldn't have done this without you.

Thank you to the San Francisco Area Chapter of Romance Writers of America. I continue to be amazed at this incredible group of authors who offer their unwavering support. My books wouldn't be where they are without you!

Last, but certainly not least, I continue to be thankful to my wonderful family for all their support. I know I'm missing out on a lot of sparkling conversations but I know you understand when I have to pay attention to those pesky voices inside my head. I love you with all my heart.

ONE

London 1808

LADY GWENDOLYN MARIE WORTHINGTON strode across the floor of her brother's study, carelessly threw her bonnet onto a high backed leather chair, and crossed her arms. The missive she held in her hand had driven all thoughts of a trip to the milliner with her friend Lady Calliope out of her head. Her shoe tapped a rapid staccato on the wooden floorboards. Her brother remained indifferent to her demand for his attention whilst he continued writing. The insufferable lout did not even have the decency to acknowledge her presence in his pursuit to finish his correspondence. She cleared her throat, hoping to gain his notice.

He continued whatever business he was attending to without a pause, except to say, in a barely civil and flat monotone, "You did not knock." His disinterest in her presence served as a reminder of his place within his household, as if she could ever forget she was subject to his directives.

Her brother had had the arrogance to send a servant to deliver his note to her bedroom. He should have come there himself to speak with her, given the news he wished to impart. She tossed the crumbled parchment onto his desk. He, in turn, swatted it aside like it was nothing but a pesky insect.

"You have been given your instructions, Gwendolyn. We have nothing further to discuss."

"Do not take that tone with me, Edmond. You may hold our father's title, but that in no way gives you leave to treat me as if I must comply with demands such as these," she fumed. Where had her carefree older brother of years past gone? Surely some measure of the young man she had adored in their youth lurked behind the expressionless mask of this unfeeling cad before her?

Edmond Gerard Worthington, 9th Duke of Hartford, set his quill down. The blue eyes he at last bothered to turn upon her were just as cold as his voice. Since he had inherited his rightful title of duke after their father's passing, along with all the responsibilities such a position held, Gwendolyn hardly recognized her brother. She swallowed hard, knowing she could not easily sway this uncaring man. Still, she had to try.

"Mother will hear of this," she warned. "She will not allow her only daughter to be wed to a man in order to fulfill some business deal made years ago."

"Mother is fully aware of the obligations that must be met. I should not have to explain how things of this nature are done, sister. Arranged marriages happen every day within the *ton*. Yours will be no exception."

"Brandon, then. Surely my younger brother cares what happens to his sister since you have made it painfully obvious you do not," Gwendolyn retorted sharply.

"He is my brother, too, if you would care to remember." Edmond sighed heavily. "Both mother and Brandon have been summoned to return to London immediately. The marriage contract was agreed years ago and bears the signatures of all parties, including your own. You would have already been wed, had it not been for father's death." Edmond leaned his elbows upon his desk, fingers forming a steeple as if contemplating his next counter to whatever argument she could muster.

She quickly thought of the first excuse that crossed her mind. "I am still in mourning," Gwendolyn declared through clenched lips.

His eyes roamed down the length of her pink floral gown and his brows rose in unsuppressed amusement. "Your mourning period is long since over, as your garments surely attest. Resign yourself to wedding Lord Sandhurst."

She stomped her foot in frustration. "Bernard Sandhurst is a lecherous old man and ancient enough to be my father." She barely held back a cry of despair. "How can you condemn me to a life with that horrible person, however long the vermin will still remain on this earth?"

"I am doing the best I can to save this family from financial ruin. You should be grateful Sandhurst will still have you, given the limited amount I could spare for your dowry. I will not be swayed in my decision, Gwendolyn, and Sandhurst can no longer be put off. He has all but stated his time waiting for you is over. He has been as patient as one could ask of a man getting on in years. You are now twenty years of age and should have been wed with children of your own by now."

Thoughts of being intimate with a man who repulsed Gwendolyn made her shudder. The few times she had had the displeasure of being alone in the same room with Lord Bernard Sandhurst, he had mauled her with his cool clammy hands. He reminded her of a fish, and an unappealing one at that.

"Edmond—"

Her brother cut her off with a wave of his hand. "Father made this decision and you must abide by it, along with the rest of us." Edmond picked up his quill and examined the tip before dipping it into the inkwell.

"You are a duke, Edmond. Surely you can pay the man off so I can find a worthy man to love." She silently pleaded with him, and, for the briefest instant, she held the smallest measure of hope he would accede to her wishes.

His piercing blue eyes leveled on her but briefly. "Love is for fools. Better to marry for wealth and a decent position in society than to lose your heart to such a frivolous emotion as love." Edmond returned to his work, the quill scratching across the parchment. The sound echoed in her head as though the missive sealed her fate. "Resign yourself to your marriage Gwendolyn. Sandhurst has made arrangements for the wedding to take place two weeks hence."

A sound escaped her that was part moan, part disbelief. "Do not do this to me, Edmond. There must be another alternative." She choked back a sob, covering her mouth to stop herself berating him for marrying her off to a man for whom she could never have even the slightest measure of affection.

Her brother looked up and Gwendolyn saw a brief instant of regret flashing in his eyes before he returned to his work. "It is done. There is nothing I can do to change the situation."

"You have no heart, Edmond. I will hate you for this until I take my last dying breath," she vowed with a raised fist.

"I know…" he whispered solemnly.

Gwendolyn ran from the study never wishing to see her brother again. A fortnight later, she was being handed into a carriage by her husband after their short emotionless wedding ceremony. Such an occasion should have been one of the happiest days of her life. Instead, her descent into hell had only just begun.

TWO

NEVILLE QUINN, EARL OF DRAYTON, took out his watch fob and made note of the time. His latest mistress, Mrs. Cassandra Vaughn, was—as usual—late for their luncheon. Although the woman was a convenient distraction from his normal daily life, perhaps it was necessary to let her find another benefactor He held no form of emotional attachment to the woman and that sentiment went both ways. It was time for him to move on to find either a more accommodating mistress who would not keep him constantly waiting, or else a wife. Heaven forbid the latter.

Neville had just about given up hope of her joining him, when he saw Cassandra enter the dining room. She was a beautiful woman and she, of course, knew it. She curved in all the right places, her hips swaying whilst she made her way towards him. She drew the attention of every gentleman in the room like an actress taking center stage in the theater, demanding their concentration.

With her blonde flaxen hair, green come-hither eyes, and honeyed smooth skin, she was a temptation most men would sell their very soul to the devil to spend even an hour with. No simpering miss was this lady. She was a woman who knew what she wanted in life, generally grabbing a hold of whatever, or whoever, took her fancy and to hell with what Society thought of her. Neville had grown tired of her being fawned over by all the young fops whenever they were out in public.

He stood, pulling out her chair, before resuming his seat. He made a motion to a nearby servant that the first course could be served. "I took the liberty of ordering for you. I have another appointment this afternoon directly after we dine," Neville stated matter-of-factly before taking a sip of his wine.

"I am sorry to be late, darling," Cassandra purred leaning closer. "Can you not put off business for the afternoon? I thought perhaps we could return to my apartment to spend a leisurely evening together."

"I am afraid I must decline, Cassandra. I chose this establishment because I hope to arrange a meeting with some gentlemen who are also dining here today."

"Really? Who are you meeting?" Her eyes scanned the room as if she were sizing up the occupants for their importance on the social ladder within the *ton*.

Neville gave the briefest of nods towards the right of their own table. "The Duke of Hartford and his brother, Lord Brandon Worthington are dining with their mother and sister." His eyes strayed to the younger lady at the table. The gentlemen's sister, Lady Sandhurst, was indeed a beautiful woman. Her husband was a lucky man.

"A duke?" Cassandra could barely contain her

excitement and he could see she was about to beg him for an introduction.

"Do not bother to ask, my dear. I hardly think introducing my mistress is appropriate with two well-bred women in attendance at the duke's table."

She pouted, as though such a ploy had ever swayed him in the past. "As if I care what they think of me." She picked up her wine glass and examined Hartford from across the room.

Neville studied her and, if he had any doubts about continuing their association, her interest in Hartford confirmed what he already knew. It was time for him to move on.

"He is currently without a mistress, if that is what you are wondering," Neville muttered off-handedly. "He may be interested in taking another, if you are drawn to him." Their lunch arrived and Neville began to eat, not bothering to wait for Cassandra's answer, since she was entirely engrossed in studying Hartford.

She continued her perusal of the man across the room before finally setting her glass down. Absentmindedly, she twirled the crystal stem between her long delicate fingers as it rested upon the table. At last, she gave a heavy sigh before she picked up her fork and proceeded to push her food around her plate. "You could cast me off that easily, Drayton? Do you not hold even the smallest increment of affection for me within that icy heart of yours?"

He wiped his mouth with a napkin before leaning back in his chair, replying quietly so their conversation would not be overheard by those nearby. "I am hardly passing you off to anyone, Cassandra. It is entirely your choice whom you plan to take as your next lover."

"Will you not miss me?"

Neville suppressed a chuckle. "Let us not play games, my dear. You and I both agreed we would not claim any emotional attachments in our relationship, especially when we decided to go our separate ways."

"You could, at the very least, feign a touch of sorrow at our parting to mend my bruised ego," Cassandra replied. She gave him a small smile, proof that she was little grieved at ending their association.

"You will hardly be lacking for company, nor money to survive," Neville continued, careful not to allow any hint that he had grown fond of her. "Your late husband ensured you would be well taken care of before his early demise, and I will deposit a large sum into your bank account that should see to your needs for some time."

"That is generous of you, Neville," she murmured softly, surprising him by the use of his given name. She reached out for his hand, giving it a pat. "Thank you."

He took her hand, raising it to his lips. "You are welcome, Cassandra. Never let it be said I did not settle my accounts."

"I would be lying if I declared I did not enjoy these past many months together. However will I get along without you to keep me amused?"

Neville laughed. "Oh, I am sure you will think of something, my dear."

Cassandra joined in with his merriment. "Yes, I suppose you have that aright. You always did know me so well and no matter what life deals me, I always tend to land on my... well... feet."

His brow rose at her insinuation and Neville had no doubt Cassandra would have another lover warming her bed before the week was out.

He rose when Cassandra bade him farewell after they had finished dining and waved his hand, calling for his bill. As he returned to his seat to wait to sign for his meal, his gaze moved across the room to land on Lady Sandhurst. Apparently, she had been looking in his direction as well, for their eyes met.

He held her stare. How could he not when he had been admiring her beauty just a short while ago? He did not dally with women whose husbands were living, and certainly not one who was associated with a potential business associate. The last thing he needed was some man breathing down his neck challenging him to a duel, and that most assuredly included her brothers as well as her husband.

To say she was beautiful would not have done the lady justice. She was young, perhaps no more than twenty. Her light brown hair was swept up into a pleasing coiffure and one long curling ringlet cascaded down her left shoulder. He could not tell the color of her eyes from this distance but they were framed in a round face with a clear complexion. Neville should not let his gaze linger on those lips for long. They were meant to be kissed and kissed often.

Something about the lady continued to pull at his heart, and, for the life of him, he could not look away. She seemed sad, and he could only ponder the cause. Why her disposition was important to him he could not say, and yet, he had a sudden desire to sweep her away and fill her days with happiness. He squashed down the notion of what he would like to do with her nights.

They continued staring, one to the other, and he watched in fascination as her chest rose and fell as if she were attempting to catch her breath. Neville had been tempted long enough and he gave into the impulse by offering her the slightest of nods. She must have at last come to her senses at his gesture, for she quickly turned away, but not before Neville witnessed a lovely blush rising to color her cheeks.

He signed his name to his bill and sat back to finish his wine. Hartford and his family appeared as though they, too, were about finished with their meal. It would be but a few minutes more before he was formally introduced to the very lovely Lady Sandhurst. He prayed his heart could withstand the encounter. He had the uncanny feeling he was about to lose it to a woman who was, unfortunately, already wed.

THREE

$\mathcal{G}$ WENDOLYN PEEKED THROUGH lowered lashes at the man who had held her attention. She had not meant to be caught staring at him but she could in no way pull her gaze from his. With a single glance, her heart fell, silently crying at the injustice of it all. No man should be so handsome, nor should she experience a connection with a complete stranger clear on the other side of the room. She gazed into the depths of her tea wondering if perhaps it was laced with something that caused her infatuation with a stranger.

She had watched his companion leave their table and Gwendolyn needed to stifle a satisfied smile the moment he was left alone. His clothes suggested he was wealthy, for they were immaculate. His hair was a deep rich auburn and she could see where the light of the dining room reflected the hints of red within the depths of his locks. His eye color could not be determined from this distance but that did not matter in the least. He was the first man who had ever made her heart flip end over end. Such an emotion certainly never happened with her husband and she knew it never would.

"Gwendolyn…"

Somewhere in her daydream, the warmth of a hand fell upon her arm bringing her back to reality. She looked up into the eyes of her mother. "Yes?"

"You were far away, sweeting. Are you unwell?" she asked, her features etched with concern.

"I am as well as can be expected," Gwendolyn replied, reaching out to take a sip of her tea. She should not have been surprised to find the brew as cold as her emotions had been of late.

"What is that supposed to mean, Gwen," Brandon inquired. "That bastard Sandhurst has not hurt you, has he?"

Edmond threw his napkin upon the table. "I am sure she is fine, brother, and her husband has treated her fairly."

A choked sob escaped Gwendolyn's parted lips. "As if you care what becomes of me, Hartford." She wouldn't give him the satisfaction of calling him by his given name. He lost the right to the intimacy they had shared as children when he forced her to accept her repugnant husband.

Edmond frowned. "And I would think by now you would let the rift that has grown between us heal. You are my little sister. I may not show it, but I care for you."

"If selling your sister to fulfill some obligation on a piece of paper is your idea of how you care for me, then I want no part of it," she said reaching for the teapot to pour herself another cup.

"You gave your consent, if you recall," Hartford growled under his breath before reaching for his wine.

"As if anyone could ever say 'no' to father once he made up his mind about something," she fumed.

"Children, enough is enough. This was supposed to be a pleasant luncheon with all three of you together for the first time in months. Can you not at least get along until we finish our meal?" their mother begged.

"I believe I have lost my appetite," Gwendolyn murmured pushing her plate away. From the corner of her eye, she saw her mystery man rise and begin making his way in their direction. He was taller than she expected, with broad shoulders. She turned to her younger brother. "Brandon, will you escort me home. I believe I need some fresh air and would not mind the walk. Hartford can take mother home in his carriage."

"Of course, Gwen," Brandon said, standing, "but I first need to speak with a gentleman who was to see us here after our lunch to arrange a meeting. Here he is now. May I present Lord Neville Quinn, Earl of Drayton? Drayton, it is my pleasure to introduce you to my mother, the Duchess of Hartford, and my sister, Lady Sandhurst. You know Hartford, of course."

"Ladies, a pleasure to make your acquaintance," Lord Drayton declared, bowing. The deep baritone of his voice went straight to Gwendolyn's heart. So this was the Earl of Drayton, a viscount's son who had astounded Society when the King granted him his current title in thanks for investment advice.

"Brandon was just about to escort my sister home," Edmond announced.

Lord Drayton turned towards her with a kind smile. Hazel. His eyes were a gorgeous shade of hazel. "Nothing serious I hope," he inquired politely.

Gwendolyn gulped, trying to find her voice. "No, nothing serious, my lord."

Silence stretched until Edmond spoke up, taking out his watch fob and noting the time. "Perhaps we could meet at White's in, say, an hour's time. That should give Brandon ample time to walk Gwendolyn home. That is, if you are still available. We can always reschedule if you have other plans."

"No, I have no previous engagements for the evening."

"Then we shall see you there. Mother, are you ready?" Edmond asked, rising and holding out his arm to escort her.

Gwendolyn felt Brandon take her elbow as they began to make their way out to the street. She could feel Lord Drayton right behind her and her treacherous heart began pounding in her chest like the fleet hooves of a deer pursued by the hunt. She was pleasantly surprised by his next words.

"Do you mind if I walk with you?" Lord Drayton inquired. "I would not mind the fresh air and the stroll would do me good after my meal."

Brandon patted him on the back. "By all means, join us. I could use the company after I see my sister home."

They fell into step, the three of them, side by side on the walkway. She would have enjoyed his banter with her brother as they strolled, but she was worried about returning home with a stranger in attendance. Sandhurst would not be pleased. She began to pray he would not be home.

FOUR

*L*ORD BERNARD SANDHURST loosened his cravat and made his way to his study with an uneasy gait. This damn gout was barely tolerable today and a good stiff drink would ease his suffering. He called out for brandy knowing his butler, Hollis, would see to the matter. Making his way to his desk, he spotted the correspondence he had barely begun. He would need to see the matter completed so it could be delivered soon.

He eased his girth into the leather chair and wondered how his breeches had become so tight. He would need to have a word with his tailor. It was obvious the man should be taken to task for not sewing his attire to the proper measurements.

A discreet knock at the door heralded Hollis as he entered carrying a tray with a decanter of amber liquor. The butler had barely poured a much-needed dose of spirits before Bernard was reaching for the crystal.

"Where is Lady Sandhurst?" Bernard inquired. Sitting

back in his chair, he closed his eyes, savoring the brandy as it made its way down his throat.

"If you would recall, sir, she had a luncheon appointment with her family. You were invited to attend but declined," Hollis said, his voice flat and unemotional as always as if to ensure no sentiment could be perceived from his tone.

"Ah, yes, with her mother and brothers, if I remember correctly. I would much prefer to be at the club than to be visiting with the in-laws."

"Of course, my lord. Will there be anything else?"

"See to your duties, Hollis. When my wife returns, send her to me," Bernard ordered, waving off the servant. He had more important matters to attend than to converse with the help.

"As you wish, sir," Hollis answered before he left the room and closed the door.

With his solitude once more assured, Bernard opened the desk drawer and pulled out a small miniature portrait of his wife. He had it commissioned right after they wed. He had held such hopes for this marriage, but once again he had taken a bride he could not even bed. He could not comprehend why he could not perform the most basic deed of rising to the occasion, and he blamed the woman in the portrait, who stared back at him with mocking eyes.

He still remembered his first wife's hysterical laughter on their wedding night when she rejoiced her maidenhood would be safe from her husband. Gwendolyn may not have dared the same reaction but he could see for himself she was just as relieved at his failure to bed her.

A snarl of outrage burst from Bernard's lips and he threw the miniature across the room where it bounced off the floor and landed in the hearth. He would be damned before he would allow Gwendolyn to take a lover as his first wife had done. His first wife and her child had died during the pregnancy, and for that he was grateful. At least he did not have to claim her bastard child as his own to save face in the eyes of Society.

Being a widower had also given him the opportunity to take another wife. He watched the miniature in mild disinterest as the frame and painting quickly caught fire until it disintegrated into nothing but ash.

Surely his inadequacy was all Gwendolyn's fault. As a young man, first visiting a brothel, he had realized he was not to blame for his impotency, which clearly resulted from a natural distaste for the unclean vessels on offer. And his first wife had proved to be just as much of a whore. No wonder he could not desire her.

Gwendolyn was pure; he had observed her for long enough to be sure of it. But she obviously did not try in earnest to arouse his manhood. He must see the deed done. If he did not impregnate her soon, he would become the laughing stock of the *ton* with no heir to inherit his life's work!

The sound of the townhouse door closing announced his wife's arrival home. Downing the remainder of his drink, he rose from the chair and hobbled towards the door. No time like the present to see the matter done. They had been married close to six months' and he had attempted many times to bed his wife, and failed. Surely today would be different.

He stopped short when he entered the foyer and saw she was not alone. Her brother Brandon he tolerated because he was family. The tall stranger, who stood next to his brother-in-law, was too good looking. Bernard had a moment of envy knowing his physical appearance would never be a match for the three young people now entering his home.

He plastered a false smile of welcome on his face. No sense giving Worthington any cause to report to Hartford that he was not treating the duke's sister as he should.

"My dear wife, I am so glad you have returned," Bernard grinned. He came to Gwendolyn, put his arm around her waist bringing her close, and placed a loving kiss upon her cheek. She flinched within his embrace, but inwardly he was satisfied he claimed the beautiful woman as his own.

Brandon stepped forward. "Lord Sandhurst, may I introduce Lord Drayton, a business associate of mine and my brother?"

Drayton held out his hand and Bernard unwilling detached himself, knowing he could not ignore a guest of the peerage in his home. "A pleasure to make your acquaintance, Lord Drayton," Bernard managed to murmur as they shook hands. "Welcome to our home."

"Thank you, Lord Sandhurst," Drayton answered with a nod.

Was it Bernard's imagination or did Drayton and his wife exchange a knowing look? His first wife must have tainted his thinking, for he knew Gwendolyn would in no way betray their marriage vows. They may not have consummated the marriage, but he knew her character. No matter the distance between them, she was in no way similar to his first wife.

"May I offer you gentleman a drink?" Bernard cordially asked, although he would rather be upstairs with Gwendolyn than entertaining her brother and his business associate.

"I am afraid we must decline, Sandhurst," Brandon replied politely. "We have another engagement."

Gwendolyn placed her hand on her brother's arm. "Will you not stay a while, Brandon?" She looked pleading, as if she would beg her brother to stay.

Her brother kissed her cheek. "You know I cannot, Gwen. We have to meet Edmond, but I will call upon you on the morrow. Perhaps we could go for a ride in the park, if you would care to accompany me."

"I will look forward to it." Her softly whispered words barely hid the disappointment in her voice.

"Until then," Brandon said, and turned away towards the door.

Drayton bowed. "Lady Sandhurst, it was indeed a pleasure to meet you."

Gwendolyn gave a short curtsey. "And you as well, Lord Drayton."

She hovered near the door watching the pair disappear down the street. When she closed the door, she leaned her forehead against the wood for a moment before turning to meet her husband's eyes. She took a deep heavy breath.

Bernard's eyes narrowed whilst he watched her compose and resign herself to what was coming. "Upstairs, now, and await me in my chamber. I will be up shortly."

He watched her flee up the stairway as fast as her feet could sweep her away. Bernard followed at the slower pace his foot demanded of him. By God, he would accomplish today what he could not manage all these many months, or die trying.

FIVE

EVILLE WAS PRACTICALLY running to keep up with Brandon Worthington. The man's stride was almost a run. He fled as if he was possessed and was attempting to escape from whatever demon was controlling him.

"Eh gads, man, will you slow down," Neville demanded, reaching out to pull on Worthington's arm. "Elsewise I will need to stop at my townhouse to refresh myself before we head to White's." The man looked on him as if he had no idea what Neville had been saying.

"What?" he snapped angrily.

"What the devil is the matter that you feel the need to sprint all the way to White's?"

Worthington stopped, rubbing his hand across the back of his neck. He then proceeded to look up and down the empty street. "I should not say anything. It is a family matter." They resumed their walk at a more leisurely pace, but Worthington was clearly still fuming.

Neville understood the importance of family but also had an inkling about what Worthington referred to. "It is your sister, is it not?" he inquired as politely as possible.

Worthington once again halted in steps. "Was it that obvious?

"No, not to the casual observer, I suppose. But even I could see Lady Sandhurst is not happy in her marriage."

"He is making her life miserable. I told Hartford to pay Sandhurst off and let Gwen choose her own husband. My brother, in no uncertain terms, told me their union would proceed as scheduled. Even my mother could not sway him. He would not give his reasons, only that our father had demanded it of him on his death bed."

"Lord Sandhurst was not what I expected. Not that it is any of my business, of course."

"They wed six months ago. In that time, I have watched my dear sweet sister become a meek little mouse and not the vibrant young woman I grew up with. It is almost as if the old coot has stolen her youth. I am afraid she will become an old woman before her time."

"You are exaggerating, Lord Brandon. Really, she is hardly old and has a full life ahead of her."

"Not with Sandhurst as her husband. She rarely leaves the house. I only suggested tomorrow's outing because I knew he would not prevent her going out if the invitation was offered in front of another. He can be a gentleman when he is in public. In private, it is another matter, or so I suspect, though Gwen does not complain."

"Tell me he does not beat her," Neville responded. His fists opened and closed at his side with the thoughts of any man taking advantage of a woman in such a manner.

"No, not that I am aware of, and yet I am not sure if my

sister would let me know if he did. She is a proud woman who is attempting to make the most of a marriage she did not want."

"Most marriages are arranged. Hers will not be the first where the couple were not compatible or did not share a common accord."

"You may have that aright, but she has told me she will never come to care for the man. She may be stuck with him but her heart, at least, belongs to no one but herself. Her words… not mine."

"I am sorry your sister is so discontented. Everyone deserves at least the smallest measure of happiness in their life," Neville murmured as they continued their walk.

They strolled for several blocks in silence until Worthington once more stopped on the walk, sliding a conspiratorial look at Neville from the corners of his eyes. "Meet us in the park on the morrow," Worthington urged.

"I beg your pardon?"

"The park. Meet us there."

"Whatever for?" Neville was almost afraid to hear Worthington's reasoning.

"For the sheer pleasure of seeing my sister smile."

Neville chuckled. "What makes you think I am the man to make your sister smile?"

"What, am I blind, or did not the two of you share a moment today during our luncheon?" Worthington asked staring at Neville almost as though he had read the very thoughts in his head. Whatever he saw prompted another smile of satisfaction.

Neville was at a loss for words. "I do not interfere nor become involved with married women."

"I am not asking you to take her as your mistress,

Drayton. I just thought you could make her feel… well… alive again. I feel somehow responsible for not coming to her aid before she was married, especially knowing what an oaf Sandhurst was. When we were younger, I admired Gwendolyn and I have never wanted to see her so unhappy. I believe you could brighten up her life, at least for a little while."

"She is your sister." Neville stated, thinking he was somewhat afraid to spend too much time with the very lovely Gwendolyn Sandhurst. Afraid of what might happen to his lack of better judgement to stay away. Afraid of what could happen to his heart if she ended up claiming some small part of it.

Worthington laughed merrily. "What of it? Did you not just say everyone deserves a bit of happiness. Help me make my sister know she is a desirable woman. Surely I was not mistaken? You find her beautiful."

Neville frown. "I am not sure I should be admitting such to her brother, of all people. This is a most unusual request, especially since you barely know me."

"Ha! I knew it," Worthington beamed, ignoring Neville's objections. "Tell me you will join us at the park tomorrow and assist me with my plan. You can feign you just came upon us."

Neville was not sure how he had been cornered into such an agreement but he gave his consent. Whilst Worthington chatted on about how and when to meet, Neville wondered what had become of his sanity. What the devil had he just gotten himself into and—better yet—how was he going to get himself out?

SIX

THE SILENCE BETWEEN Gwendolyn and Bernard stretched to fill the dining room. This morning, she could barely stand the sight of the man who had humiliated her yesterday. Another failed attempt at taking her maidenhead had seemed to last hours before it ended with Bernard cursing her to the very devil and ordering her from his bedroom. She could not leave the room fast enough to find sanctuary behind her own locked door.

The sounds coming from his end of the breakfast table were so loud she wondered if the man had ever been given lessons on eating with his mouth closed. Gwendolyn held back a grimace whilst he continued shoveling eggs into his mouth. He acted as if he were consuming the last meal he would ever be given, or someone was about to take away his plate, half unfinished. Disgusted with his lack of manners, she gave a silent word of thanks that at least such a display was not in public. She could barely stand the sounds Bernard made whilst his lips smacked at his meal, nor did she want to think about the sight of her husband's growing girth. If he did not take better care of himself, she would be a widow by the end of the year.

Their marriage had been a far cry from her youthful dreams. If only she could have found some friendly common ground with Bernard. At least that would be some form of consolation but even that was denied her. He only demanded to be in her company when he deemed himself ready to consummate their marriage again. He failed day after day, insisting it was her fault. Gwendolyn wondered if there really was something wrong with her. Seeing him clothed was at least tolerable. Seeing him naked was an entirely different matter. Too disgusting to put into words.

She shuddered whilst numerous memories assaulted her mind. Still, she must be doing something wrong, but how was she to know what could be the cause? Her mother had mentioned the act was a pleasant one, although how she could possibly find it so with Bernard was beyond her comprehension. She must be the only woman known to mankind who remained a virgin after being married for the longest six months of her life.

Bernard. After their wedding, he had asked her to call her by his first name, but her tongue choked on the intimacy. Perhaps if she used it enough in her thoughts, it would become natural.

A loud belch interrupted her musings, causing Gwendolyn to raise her eyes from her plate to peer at Bernard who was rising from the other side of the table. "I may be late this eve," he muttered off handedly. His uneven gait when he began to leave the room caused him to move at a slower pace.

"Perhaps we should call a doctor to look at your foot,

Lord Sandhurst," Gwendolyn stated. While she may not care for the man, she hated to see anyone in pain.

"Mind your own business. If I am in need of medical attention, then I shall have a physician sent for. I do not need some sawbones either taking my foot or bleeding me to death." His tone told her in no uncertain terms to let the matter drop.

Gwendolyn shrugged. "I was only trying to help, my lord. If you do not wish to heed my council, then you can hobble about on a sore foot. You should be resting, not walking about when your leg should probably be elevated."

He paused as if he would reconsider but he was a stubborn old fool. "I have business to attend to at my club. You should stay inside today. It may rain."

"You forget my brother is coming to accompany me for a ride in the park. If you care to look, there is not a cloud in the sky." She waved to the open curtains, proof that the weather was fine.

Bernard scratched his head. "Ah, yes, I forgot. Give my best to your brother, then."

He did not wait for a reply and Gwendolyn was relieved to see him leave. Any moment of solitude she had in this house was always welcome.

Hollis entered from the kitchen and waved at a servant to clear Bernard's dishes. "May I get you anything else, your ladyship?"

"No, thank you, Hollis. I believe I will wait for my brother and finish my tea in the parlor." Before she knew it, Hollis was by her side assisting her with her chair. She gave him a timid smile of gratitude. "You have been so kind to me, Hollis."

He bowed and motioned for a maid to collect the tea

service. They followed behind her to set the tray near the hearth. "It is indeed a pleasure to serve you, madam."

Gwendolyn picked up her teacup and had barely finished the calming brew before Brandon was walking into the parlor. He came to her, took both her hands, and pulled her into his embrace as if he knew she was in need of a hug of reassurance, however false. Most definitely, everything would not be all right. She wrapped her arms around his waist and held on, trying her best not to let loose the tears that threatened to pour like a river from her eyes.

Brandon pulled back, holding her at arm's length and inspecting her, though for signs of what only he knew for sure. "Is something the matter, Gwen?" he asked, displeasure in his frown.

"I am fine," she managed to whisper in a somewhat shaky voice.

"You do not look it. Has he hurt you?" Brandon tipped up her chin inspecting her once more.

"No. At least not physically, but I will not go into the particulars of my marriage with you or anyone else. Let the matter rest, Brandon."

"Maybe Edmond—"

A snarl burst from her lips before she whirled away from her brother. She went to stand near the window. "Do not mention his name to me. Hartford condemned me to a loveless marriage when he could well have paid the man to find himself another wife."

"He told me he had his reasons."

"I did not want to hear his reasoning then and I certainly do not wish to hear it now from either of you. It will take a miracle for me to forgive our brother for what he has done to me."

Brandon crossed the floor to place a kiss upon her forehead. "I did not mean to upset you. Let us go on our outing. It is a beautiful day outside."

"I am in a foul mood. Perhaps it would be best if you go without me," Gwendolyn pouted.

"Nonsense. I am here to get you out to enjoy the day and enjoy it we shall. I will hear no further objections from you, Gwen. Now get your parasol and let us be on our way."

Several minutes later, as Gwendolyn sat in her brother's carriage, she admitted the outing was already doing her some good. The sunshine felt wonderful and the park was filled with a multitude of people both in carriages and on horseback. She waved to her dear friend, Lady Calliope Powell, who rode by on a pretty dapple grey mare with her groom following close behind. She had known Callie since childhood and had missed her company of late. She had been meaning to call upon her, but Bernard did not approve of her making calls without him, and he did not care to socialize unless with business contacts. Since she wed, Gwendolyn felt like a recluse deprived of seeing any of her old friends, and alone most nights while her husband attended to his commercial interests.

Brandon continued to chatter away as though he had not noticed she had become lost in thought. From his tone, he was obviously attempting to change her melancholy mood.

"Well, look who else came to enjoy the park today," Brandon declared merrily, waving his hand.

Gwendolyn saw many familiar faces as she looked about. "There are any number of people around, Brandon. Is there someone in particular I should see besides Callie who just rode by?"

Brandon turned to her with a bright smile. "Why it is

none other than Lord Drayton, of course."

Her head swiveled in the direction her brother was motioning, and, sure enough, Lord Drayton was making his way towards them on a magnificent brown horse with flowing black mane and tail. A sudden lump formed in her throat, making it difficult to swallow. Her heartbeat increased the closer he came, and she wondered if she would even be able to form a word, let alone a complete sentence once he came abreast of their carriage.

The air rushed from her lungs confirming her worst fears. Neville Quinn, or more correctly, Lord Drayton, was a dangerous distraction, and her treacherous heart would surely wind her up in more trouble than she was ready for at this time of her life.

Lord Drayton reined in his horse and tipped his hat. "Good day to you, Worthington. Lady Sandhurst, you are looking particularly lovely this fine morning." His grin could only be termed roguish.

Did the man have to speak, let alone use flattery that was like an arrow piercing straight to her heart? She tried to form some kind of reply but her mouth went suddenly dry. For the life of her, she could not think of a single syllable to utter. *Goodness, he will think me a complete fool.*

SEVEN

HE YOUNG WOMAN was completely charming. After opening and closing her mouth several times, she at last gave Neville a slight nod of acknowledgment.

"Lord Drayton," she murmured softly before a blush crept up her beautiful face. The effect was most becoming and it pleased him to think he had flustered her, since he had much the same reaction whenever she was near. Or so he was learning.

"So good to see you again, Drayton. My sister was just saying she would like to walk instead of ride in my carriage."

Gwendolyn turned wide eyes to her brother. "I was?"

Brandon laughed. "Of course you were, my dear. Would you mind walking with her, Drayton? Just tie your horse to the back and I'll manage the carriage."

"I cannot think of a better way to spend the morning than a stroll through the park with your lovely sister," Neville answered and went to tie the reins of his horse behind Worthington's carriage. He hid a smile when he overheard Lady Sandhurst's soft whisper asking her brother what he was about.

Neville returned to the side of the carriage, opened the door, and extended his hand for the lady. She hesitated only an instant before she put her gloved hand in his. It trembled beneath his fingertips and Neville had the urge to pull the glove from her hand to feel her warm skin next to his own. Their brief contact was over all too quickly when Lady Sandhurst pulled her hand from his.

"I shall return shortly. I see an acquaintance with whom I must chat. You two enjoy your stroll," Brandon announced. He flicked the reins before he had even finished his words. He and the carriage took off leaving Lady Sandhurst wearing a quizzical look.

"It appears you are stuck with me, Lord Drayton," she declared through pursed lips. Clearly she was not pleased with her brother.

"I deem it an honor to accompany you about the park, my lady."

They began to walk side by side, a familiar reminder they had just been walking together yesterday. The silence stretched and he continued to watch her from the corner of his eyes. She was doing much the same.

"It is a beautiful day, is it not, Lady Sandhurst?" Neville began, trying to find some common accord to break the tension. Was it from the fact that they should not be together, her being a married woman? Or was it that they were attracted to one another? Neville could not say.

The lady gave a small burst of laughter and Neville was once more pleased to know he was the source of her joy. "I am sure we can think of a better topic than the weather to discuss, my lord," she replied, pointing towards the clear blue sky above with a wave of her hand.

Neville joined the merriment. "I thought it could not hurt as a start for a conversation between us."

"You must forgive my brother, Lord Drayton. I do not know what has come over him that he would ask you to walk with me, which is far from appropriate." She glanced shyly at him from the corner of her eyes. "But I could not resist taking advantage of the opportunity."

Even though it should not, it pleased him to think she found him hard to resist. "You do not get out much?"

"I am afraid not and certainly never with someone who is practically a stranger."

"Then we shall have to become friends in order to calm any fears you may have," Neville answered in a husky whisper, wondering at his thoughts, let alone his impulsiveness in voicing them aloud.

Lady Sandhurst looked at him as though assessing the truthfulness of his words. "I do not fear you, Lord Drayton and certainly Brandon must trust you with my welfare, or he would never have left me in your care."

"I am sure he has only your best interest at heart."

"I suppose that remains to be seen. I have the uncanny feeling the two of you are in cahoots about something."

Neville chuckled. "A lady who is very perceptive it seems. What in the world do you think your brother and I are conspiring about?"

"I would not even try to guess at the possibilities," she murmured and Neville had the distinct feeling this woman knew exactly what Worthington was up to.

"Perhaps he just wishes you to be happy and thought an outing in the park would help."

"It will take more than a stroll to change the course of

my life, sir. I am no man's pawn to be played with like a piece on a chess board of chance."

"This is no game, Lady Sandhurst."

"I hope you are telling the truth, Lord Drayton. I am a married woman. That I am with you, without a chaperone, cannot happen again. I will not be made the subject of gossip nor ridiculed as if I was a fallen woman." Lady Sandhurst's reply was curt and to the point. Her rushed words suggested she was trying to convince herself she had done nothing wrong.

"I hold you in the highest esteem, my lady. I would not think of dishonoring you or threatening your reputation.

They continued onward, silence once more filling the empty space between them. But Neville swore he could sense the undercurrents of emotions warring within the lady next to him.

"Friends, then," she rushed on looking at him again. "We can only be friends."

"But, of course, Lady Sandhurst."

A common understanding passed between them but the zing of excitement whilst they gazed at each other was enough to cause him to lose his breath. She began to quicken her pace, almost as if she were panicking. Then the unthinkable happened. Neville watched when she began to trip and pitch forward. A startled gasp escaped her whilst her parasol flew through the air. Neville bolted forward until he found his arms filled with the very desirable body of Lady Sandhurst.

Was it possible for time to actually stand still? Nothing existed but the woman in his arms. Not the park, and certainly not any passersby who may have witnessed her falling. Everything around Neville was a blur with the exception of Gwendolyn… yes, her given name was in his mind whilst he held her.

Her eyes were a soft deep brown reminding him of the earth after a gentle rain. One of her brown tendrils of hair escaped her coiffure and Neville could not resist reaching up to tuck the silken lock behind her ear. Yet the lock seemed to have a will of its own, the end of the curling tendril wrapping itself around his finger as if taking possession of him. Her breath hitched when his fingertips skimmed across her cheek, her pupils dilated, and Neville knew she was just as affected by his touch as he.

He did not know if she was aware what moistening her lips did to him. He wanted to taste her tempting mouth until it was red and swollen from his kisses, but the park was hardly the place for such behavior, especially since he just told her that she could trust him.

Her hands grasped at the lapels of his jacket. "Lord Drayton, please," she whispered bringing him back down to earth. He began to set her on her feet only to hear her gasp with pain.

"You cannot stand?" he inquired, concerned for her welfare.

She tried again, only to fall back against him. "I believe I have twisted my ankle."

"Then I am afraid we will have to put our newfound friendship to the test, my lady," Neville declared, scooping her up in his arms.

"Lord Drayton, what on earth are you doing? Put me down this instant, sir."

"I am afraid I must decline, Lady Sandhurst. You are injured and, as a gentleman, I cannot in good conscious allow you to attempt to walk and incur further harm. You will just have to humor me whilst we find your brother and then a doctor."

"What will people think seeing us like this?" she asked, wide eyes darting to those around who may be watching them. Her arms wrapped around his neck bringing them closer. She smelled like the scent of summer. Sweet jasmine, if he were not mistaken.

"I do not give a damn what they think, madam, and neither should you," he warned her.

When she rested her head upon him, Neville knew in no uncertain terms the ice surrounding his heart had just cracked wide open. May God help him when he would have to return her to her damned husband.

Bernard rose from his chair, satisfied with the arrangements that had just concluded. "Keep me apprised of your findings. Remember... whenever she leaves the house, I want her followed everywhere she goes. I will expect a full detailed report. You will be compensated according to the terms we just agreed upon."

"You can count on me and my firm, your lordship."

"Just be discrete. I do not need Society thinking I cannot keep track of my wife's whereabouts, nor do I need the gossipmongers to besmirch my good name."

"Of course, my lord."

Bernard shook hands to seal their deal and left the man's office. There were still plenty of hours left in the day to head to his club. He was in need of a good stout drink and he would enjoy the remainder of the evening knowing Gwendolyn would not step foot out of the manor without his knowing what she did. Sometimes having a young beautiful wife had its drawbacks, but he would ensure he was not betrayed by another wife having an affair. If he could not have her in his bed, then by damned no other man would either.

EIGHT

$\mathcal{G}$ WENDOLYN COULD FEEL each breath Lord Drayton took. Could feel the corded muscles of his arms as he carried her with ease, as though she weighed no more than a babe. Being this close to him, she could see the slight stubble beginning to grow on his face as the morning progressed.

She inhaled the scent of spice that seemed so much a part of him. She almost sighed in pleasure to be this close to a gentleman who seemed intent on protecting her. So this is what it felt like to sense that someone actually cared for her well-being, someone who was not her family, that is. Being at last able to finally *feel...* it must be fate playing a cruel joke on her. The warmth of muscled chest pressed against her caused a tingling sensation to race throughout her entire body. Seeing the flecks of green light up in the depths of his hazel eyes when he looked down upon her made her warm. And when her heart somersaulted endlessly, she rejoiced knowing he was the cause.

He was a stranger, more or less, and yet, perhaps, not a stranger after all. How could these bizarre sensations be so wrong when her heart was telling her everything about him was so right? Yet wrong they were, for she was already spoken for. Nothing could come of this emotional attachment she felt for Neville Quinn. How many times would she need to repeat that mantra to herself?

"I am sorry I am such a burden to you, Lord Drayton," Gwendolyn murmured in a soft hush. "Perhaps you could just put me down on the bench over there and then go find Brandon. I am sure I will be fine until your return."

"You are not a burden." His voice was firm in his resolve to continue to carry her to her brother's carriage.

"I highly doubt you are used to carrying a damsel in distress for several furlongs, my lord." She smiled up at him and he returned her smile with a roughish grin that would have knocked her off her feet had she been standing.

"You are as light as a feather, my lady, and I will not leave you to fend for yourself for even one instant. You will just have to indulge me so I can at least say I did my duty as a gentleman."

"You are too kind, sir."

"Under the circumstances, perhaps you would consider calling me by my given name, at least when we are alone together." Was it her imagination or did he seem to hold his breath as he awaited her answer.

"I am not sure how many more unusual requests I can handle in one day."

He halted his pace, looked around, and immediately walked into a group of nearby trees ensuring their privacy. He set her down gently, still keeping his arms around her for support so she was not putting any weight on her injured ankle. Her hands automatically went to his chest, whether it was to keep him at a distance or to keep him close, she did not know. It did not seem to matter whatsoever. She only knew her heart told her being here with this man made everything right in the world.

He cupped her face with his free hand and she leaned into it. "Say my name, Gwendolyn."

Her breath caught in her breast hearing her own name come from his mouth; a mouth that surely awaited her kiss. His tone was low and sultry. How refreshing that a man was not demanding her consent but instead using a gentle urging.

"As you wish, Neville."

His eyes brightened with happiness and it pleased her to think she was the reason for his joy. She had never wanted to be kissed by a man more than she did at this very instant. Neville began to lean forward and she closed her eyes waiting for the sinful pleasure they would share. She was expecting his mouth to cover her own. She did not expect his lips to kiss her forehead instead before he picked her back up to resume their quest to find her brother.

Disappointment must have registered on her face because Neville began laughing. "Do not think I am not tempted, Gwendolyn, but this is not the place to steal your kisses, no matter how much I want to."

"I do not know what you are talking about," she fumed, managing to hide her laughter, or so she thought.

"Oh, yes you do, my lady. When you become cross with me, as you are now, you may call me Drayton."

Gwendolyn could not contain her mirth. "And will I become cross with you often, Drayton?"

He laughed and the sound went straight to her heart.

"Most assuredly, my lady. I can only imagine it will become a regular occurrence during the course of our relationship."

"I have the distinct impression our association may very well become a battle of wills."

"I shall look forward to the duel, Gwendolyn."

She gazed up at him shyly. She swore his eyes were sparkling like the brightest of diamonds. "As will I, Neville."

Espying, Brandon off in the distance, Neville let out a whistle to gain her brother's attention. "Your ride will be here in a moment, my lady."

She dared to finger the lapel of his jacket. "Neville?"

Those hypnotizing eyes of his looked upon her as though he were searching into her soul. "Yes, Gwendolyn?" he murmured huskily causing her to shiver. He brought her closer, most likely thinking she was chilled.

She had to ask the question that was in the forefront of her mind, even though she knew she should have nothing further to do with Neville from this moment forward. "What exactly is this relationship of ours?"

His hazel eyes appeared somewhat sad. "I have no idea, my dear."

Any further conversation was cut off as Brandon brought the carriage around and she was deposited within. Neville grumbled something about accompanying them to see that she was well cared for. The ride to her townhouse was almost unbearable. She could not take her gaze from Neville's and all she wanted to do was throw herself onto the other seat to sit beside him. Whatever in the world had she gotten herself in to and worse yet, what was she going to do now?

NINE

$\mathcal{B}$ ERNARD'S CARRIAGE DREW up to his townhouse. What the devil was going on within his home? His coachman needed to pull past his own front door due to the two carriages and several unfamiliar horses that were in his way, preventing him entrance to his residence.

The footman opened the door and let down the step. Bernard began hobbling down the walk, his temper and disposition growing fouler the closer he got to his own front steps. He could not believe his wife would dare to entertain without his consent. She knew how he felt about such things.

His hat was taken as he entered, and he heard several conversations coming from the parlor. Slowly and painfully, he made his way in that direction. His gaze swept the room and he was none too pleased to see Lord Drayton hovering near the window. Gwendolyn's friend, Lady Calliope, was standing next to him, which would explain the groom outside waiting for her. He had never cared for the woman, and with good reason. She always looked at him as though he was not good enough for Gwendolyn.

Seeing a physician attending his wife prompted a moment of concern. This should have been the first thing he had noticed but the group of healthy thriving young people had set his thoughts raging with jealousy.

"Sandhurst, we were just about to send a messenger to your club," Brandon said, still holding his sister's hand, which he raised to his lips before letting it go. "I called for Dr. Thornberry to attend her, him being our family physician."

Bernard nodded to the doctor who rose from his patient's side. "What happened?' he inquired with furrowed brow.

"I had a misstep, my lord, on the park path. My own foolish clumsiness, I am afraid, from not watching where I was walking" Gwendolyn replied in a hushed tone.

"I thought you were going for a carriage ride?" Bernard asked, his eyes moving from one individual to the other before returning to look upon his wife. Her eyes also darted about the room. Why did she appear guilty, or was he just imagining things?

"Well… I…" Her hesitation made him once more wonder what the woman had been doing with her day.

"And…" Bernard prompted her to finish whatever excuse she was about to make.

"I… I decided I wanted to walk for a bit in the beautiful sunshine," she replied with a timid smile.

"I see." He turned toward her brother. "You were supposed to be looking after her." Bernard waved a fist in Worthington's direction.

"It is hardly Brandon's fault I fell, my lord," Gwendolyn

insisted, quite sternly.

Bernard glared at her, then caught sight of Worthington's raised eyebrows and forced his voice into an affectional tone. "You cannot blame me for my concern, Lady Sandhurst," he chided, before leveling his gaze upon the physician. "Well, doctor? What is her prognosis?"

Dr. Thornberry finished putting various items back into his satchel. Closing it with a snap he began making his way towards the door. "Lady Sandhurst will be just fine. She has a minor sprain and should stay off her foot for at least a week."

Worthington made his way toward the doctor to shake his hand. "Thank you for coming so swiftly."

"I have been in service to your family for many years and am always at your disposal. Now if you will excuse me, I have another patient I must see to across town. Lord Sandhurst, a pleasure to make your acquaintance sir, despite the circumstances. Please send for me if her ladyship has need of me or the swelling does not begin to go down in a few days."

The physician left, and an awkward silence reigned until Worthington waved at Drayton. "Shall we also be on our way, Drayton?"

Drayton's gaze briefly travelled to Gwendolyn who continued to recline on the sofa. He gave her a low bow. "I hope you are well soon, Lady Sandhurst. Good day." He left without a further word.

The remaining guest in Bernard's home was looking upon him with a fair amount of contempt. He would soon deal with that. "You may take your leave as well." His voice sounded harsh, even to his own ears, not that he cared what the woman thought of him.

She had the audacity to raise her chin in such a defiant manner that Bernard's anger rose to new heights. "I will stay with my friend to ensure she recovers," Calliope answered, coming to stand near Gwendolyn.

"No, you will not. I am more than capable of taking care of my wife and seeing to her needs," he roared. Lowering his voice, he told her, "You are not welcome here."

"Lord Sandhurst, she is my dearest friend," Gwendolyn protested, making a grab for Calliope's hand. The two women held on to one another as though their lives depended on them staying together.

Bernard frowned. "Lady Calliope has made it perfectly clear what she thinks of me and our marriage. Even now, she can barely stand there with a civil look upon her face."

"My lord," Calliope attempted but Bernard held up his hand to silence her. She snapped her lips shut.

"Save your words, madam, for they will fall upon deaf ears. I repeat... you are not welcome in this house. Say your goodbyes to my wife and get out." Bernard turned his back on the women, but would not allow them any form of privacy. As he stood at the window staring out at the busy street, he heard the two ladies exchange broken whispers. Then the front door slammed and he watched Calliope make a hasty retreat to her horse. With the obtrusive woman gone, he left his wife, not caring she wept silently at the loss of her friend.

TEN

$\mathcal{N}$EVILLE FINISHED TYING his cravat and held out his arms as his valet, Jacob, helped him with his jacket. His man began brushing some imaginary speck off his shoulders. Neville was positive there was not anything there that needed attention but Jacob liked to ensure his master was dressed his finest at all times.

"Will I do, Jacob," Neville asked, already knowing the answer.

"The lady should be pleased with your appearance, my lord."

Moving across the room, he went to retrieve a stickpin with a small emerald. Placing it within his neck cloth, he turned back to his servant who had seen to his needs since he was a young man barely out of the school room. "I was not aware I mentioned I was dining this evening with a lady."

"An assumption on my part, my lord, considering you have changed the choice of your garments three times," he

46

answered handing over Neville's hat.

"Why do I put up with you, Jacob?" Neville smirked knowing he would never discharge the older man. He had become like family.

"Most likely because I am far too old to find another position, sir, and you take it upon yourself to continue to need me. I sincerely doubt another could guess your desires before you voice them."

"No doubt you are correct as usual, Jacob."

"I will call for your carriage, Lord Drayton."

Neville stared at his reflection after Jacob left. What the devil was he doing? He must be insane to be agreeing to a private dinner meeting with Gwendolyn. It had been close to a month since he had last seen her and in all that time there was rarely a day when he had not thought of her.

He had last been in her company that fateful day at the park. He had willingly gone back to her townhouse with Worthington who had called for the family physician immediately upon seeing his sister settled in her parlor. The house had begun to get busier by the second when several maids entered carrying refreshments. Even Gwendolyn's friend made an appearance and been introduced. The doctor had arrived with hardly any time passing and told Gwendolyn to stay off her ankle for at a minimum a week. Thankfully nothing was broken, just bruised, and would heal quickly with rest.

Lord Sandhurst's arrival had dampened the already gloomy air in the room, since concern for Gwendolyn was in the forefront of everyone's mind. Clearly he was not pleased his wife had been injured, let alone his house was full of strangers. Sandhurst had started to chastise Worthington when Gwendolyn intervened. But the look the man tossed his wife for voicing a reprimand, apparently coming to his senses, caused Neville to shudder.

Bernard had continued to look between his wife and Neville as though he could read their minds. It became more and more uncomfortable in the man's presence, almost to the point where Neville wondered if his face plainly revealed his feelings for another man's wife. The short time they had known each other did not seem to matter in the least, as far as he was concerned. Sandhurst had made it clear Neville was not welcomed in his home, nor was anyone else for that matter. One of the hardest things he had ever done was to leave with Worthington. Neville could tell their marriage was not an amicable one. At least Gwendolyn was not alone in that house since Lady Calliope had remained.

He shook his musings from his head. He must be insane to be going through with tonight's engagement. Worthington had arranged the dinner between them. Worthington's coach was to pick up his sister and bring her back to his townhouse. Neville was to be already in attendance by the time she arrived.

He checked his watch fob and realized he would be late if he did not leave at once. He left his bedroom and made his way into the foyer where Jacob handed him his hat and opened the door. "Have a good evening, Lord Drayton."

"Thank you, Jacob. No need to wait up for me," he said, giving a nod to his butler Henry who hovered near the door.

"As you wish, my lord," they answered in unison.

Neville made his way to his waiting carriage and, once he was settled, the conveyance was set into motion. The clip clop of the horse's hooves as they made their way over the cobblestone road sounded as if someone was trying to knock some sense into his head without any success. He was a fool to be meeting her. Worthington was a fool for suggesting the dinner take place at his home, and Gwendolyn was a fool for agreeing to meet him in the first place. They were all treading dangerous waters and the last thing he wanted was for Gwendolyn to be hurt with this deception of theirs. What were they thinking?

For Neville, the answer was easy, he only wanted to see her again, the rightness of it mattered not.

Neville's carriage came to a halt and he opened the door himself before sending his rig on its way to return home. The walk to the end of the block did not take long, especially since he knew Gwendolyn would arrive shortly. His conscience told him he should turn around and go home before another minute passed, but he could not stop himself from reaching for the knocker on Worthington's front door. He had to admit he was excited to see the fair lady, no matter that this whole situation was entirely wrong.

Worthington opened the door and quickly ushered Neville inside. "You made it. I knew you would not let me down." Worthington waved to a servant to come and take Neville's coat.

He shrugged out of the garment along with taking off his hat. "I have a bad feeling about this, Worthington. Perhaps we should reconsider this plan of ours. I do not want to see Gwendolyn hurt."

Worthington patted Neville on the back. "I knew you cared for her. I could see it the minute you two set eyes upon one another."

"Of course I care for her, but, eh gads man, this has disaster written all over it. We should be meeting somewhere else besides your home. This is a ridiculous plan you have come up with. What will the servants think? What if Hartford finds out what we have been up to?"

Worthington at least had the decency to pale at the mention of his older brother. "Hartford must never find out what lengths I have gone to in order to bring you both together. He shall never forgive me, especially since I get to be the carefree brother whilst he harbors all the responsibility of his ducal title. As far as the servants are concerned, you are being paranoid, Drayton. What is wrong with a brother asking his sister over for dinner? Even her husband will think nothing of it. She will be perfectly safe here, and I will conveniently disappear to leave the two of you to your meal. You can thank me later," Worthington smirked knowingly.

"I will either thank you or throttle you. I cannot for the life of me remember why I agreed to this. And to be conspiring with the lady's own brother? I have surely lost any sense I was born with. How the evening progresses will remain to be seen, along with your fate, my friend. This has got to be one of the stupidest things I have ever done in my entire life."

"Just treat her kindly, Drayton, or you shall answer to me."

"I can only hope this does not backfire on us and her husband finds out."

"Relax. I have it all covered."

"I hope so," Neville groaned, but there was no time to change his mind as the knocker sounded again at the door and Brandon went to admit his sister.

When she entered the foyer, Neville thought she floated inside like she was on a cloud. Surely she must be one of God's own angels come down to earth to grace such unworthy mortals like him with her presence.

Any thoughts he may have had of leaving before he lost his heart vanished the instant she turned a radiant smile in his direction. Neville was lost..

ELEVEN

$\mathcal{G}$ WENDOLYN ENTERED HER brother's home with trepidation in her heart. What was she doing and why was Brandon helping her to meet with another man? In his home. As if he approved. Heaven help her!

The door shut behind her, willingly plunging her into the intrigue of the evening. There was no turning back now, although all she would need to say was she changed her mind. *Say it, Gwendolyn,* she warred with herself inside her head. *I have changed my mind.* The words whispered fleetingly across her mind, but did not form upon her lips. How could they, after her eyes met Neville's across the dimly lit foyer?

Was there actually any space between them? Gwendolyn did not think so. When Brandon took her elbow to begin escorting her down the hall, she sensed Neville's presence directly behind her.

Brandon opened the door to his study. A fire burned bright in the hearth. A table was set for two with a sideboard holding covered dishes. "I will leave you to your meal. No need for me to stay where I am not wanted," he joked good naturedly.

"Brandon, I—"

He placed a kiss upon her cheek cutting off anything else she might have said to him. "For once in your life, Gwen, do not think. Just enjoy the moment. Lord knows how much you deserve it."

The door shut behind him, leaving her alone with Neville. The draperies to the room were closed allowing the outside world no admittance to the intimate setting within. She shivered, not from fear, but more that she was actually here… with him.

"You came," his throaty words, uttered softly in her ear, had her resisting the urge to lean back into his body that was almost touching her backside.

"Yes, I came. I know I should have remained at home, but here I am." She turned to face him.

"I am pleased you decided to join me," he declared holding out his hand. "May I?"

She reached up to take his outstretched fingers. He took hers and gently tugged at her glove before putting it into his jacket. "Something for me to always remember you," he whispered, before raising her hand to place a kiss on the inside of her wrist, "not that I could ever forget you."

"Nor I you, Neville." She could feel her eyes glistening over with unshed tears. The warmth of his hand in hers was almost her undoing. Until this very moment, she had not been aware how much she craved even the gentlest of touches from another.

"Come, you must be famished," he urged, ushering her to the table. "If you will permit me, I will be your most obedient servant this evening."

"Really? Obedient? Such a vow could land you in trouble, my lord," Gwendolyn teased.

"I was in trouble the moment I first discovered you at luncheon that day, let alone when I walked through your brother's door."

"I do not regret meeting you here, Neville."

"Nor I, Gwendolyn."

Neville held out her chair and Gwendolyn sat down into the cushion. His hand came to rest lightly upon her shoulder and she reached up to give it a slight squeeze. He went to the sideboard and began putting an assortment of food upon their plates before setting hers at her place on the table. With the wine poured, they began to eat in silence for several minutes, each lost in their own thoughts.

"Tell me of yourself," Neville asked, before taking a sip of his wine.

"What is there to tell? I had a normal upbringing, most likely similar to your own. Being the daughter of a duke does have certain responsibilities or opens many doors if you have need of something."

"And what do you stand in need of now?"

Gwendolyn sighed. "That is a difficult question to answer, for there are many things I wish were different in my life. I know I should not speak of it, but my marriage is a shambles and hardly one you read about in a romance novel."

"I would not have our conversation upset you, Gwendolyn. You need not speak of your marriage," Neville replied, reaching across the table for her hand.

"How can I not? I do not mean to be a bore, but you must understand that for me to be here with you, alone, is completely out of character. I do not make a habit of late night trysts with men I barely know. Betraying my husband will surely land me in hell."

"Then we will go there together. Let me also confess I do not make a habit of stealing another man's wife. Yet, you must admit there is something between us that cannot be explained. I know you feel it, too." Neville pushed back his chair, took her hand and led her to a settee. She began to move to one side but he would have none of it. "Do not go so far away. I would have you close to me. You are mine… at least for as long as this night will allow us."

His hand continued to hold onto hers and she gave up any further protests that may have spilled from her lips. They would have been falsehoods and there was no sense lying to the man who was tearing down the last defenses to her heart.

She raised her eyes to meet his. There was so much promise hidden within the depths of those piercing hazel orbs. "I can never truly be yours, Neville, just as surely as you can never be mine."

"We have nothing but time this night, Gwendolyn," he murmured, leaning forward he pressed a kiss upon her temple.

"Time… this evening will pass too swiftly, and then I will once more be returned to the nightmare of my life."

"Then do not think of what the morrow will bring. Tonight, I will keep you safe at my side."

Gwendolyn leaned her head upon his shoulder and he put his arm around her. Safe. He was like a boat anchor keeping her grounded whilst the waves crashed against the shore, attempting to pull loose the ropes that would keep her moored to a dock. Yet, the reality of her life remained with her and her conscience would not let go of the values she had adhered to all her life.

She leaned back to look up at the most handsomest man she had ever beheld. "I cannot become your mistress, Neville," she confessed. He stroked his hand through her hair so gently she almost burst out into tears at the injustice of it all.

"I know," he whispered, before leaning down to give her their first kiss.

How could she have known just one taste would make a simple kiss so meaningful? How could she have known a kiss could be so pleasurable? How could she have known her life would change forever in the instant their breath mingled as one? She had changed, and she now knew what everyone spoke of when they said they were in love. Love… she had fallen in love with Neville the moment she had first seen him. However in the world would she live without him? More importantly, how was she supposed to return home to a husband she could not help but hate?

TWELVE

NEVILLE HELD GWENDOLYN in his arms and swore he wished never to let her go. He deepened their kiss and a fire erupted in his loins he would be hard pressed to put out. If she only knew what she did to him with the simple gesture of cupping his face, she would have run from her brother's house and never looked back. What had they gotten themselves into?

He broke off their kiss and disappointment flashed in her eyes. "Do not stop, Drayton," she murmured seductively.

Neville smiled knowing from the use of his title she was miffed at him. "I cannot take much more, my sweet Gwendolyn." He pressed forward to nibble on her pouting lower lip. "I am only a man after all, and your sweet charms will be my undoing if we continue."

She put her arms around his neck and pulled. "Just one more. Make me forget everything else but you."

Neville groaned and gave in to her demand. How could

he not, when she begged him for another kiss? He pressed her down so she was lying on the settee, but when their bodies molded together as one, her eyes flew open wide. There was no way to hide his arousal pressed intimately against her.

The grin he gave her must surely appear wicked. If he did not know better, he would have said her reaction was virginal, but surely that could not be the case? She was a married woman and must know what she was doing.

Unless… he had never heard of Sandhurst keeping a mistress, and thought the first Lady Sandhurst had died in childbirth, there were rumors that she had a lover.

Yet the tiny whimpers he heard deep in Gwendolyn's throat suggested she was familiar with passion. Or was that merely her reaction to being with him?

Neville pressed himself against Gwendolyn once more to test his theory. A gasp escaped her and she pushed against him until he sat up.

Her hand covered her mouth and he could see for himself the blush flushing her cheeks. "I am so sorry, Neville. You must think me a brazen hussy throwing myself at you like this."

"I think no such thing. As you can tell, I cannot help what you do to me, Gwendolyn. You are a very lovely woman."

Her face became even redder, clearly from embarrassment. She stood and made her way across the room to distance herself from him. "My husband would not agree with you."

"Not that we should mention him at a time like this, but I am certain your husband is pleased to have you as his wife."

"I doubt that is what I would call it, Neville. My husband has not... he cannot..." she cleared her throat and made her way to the fire.

Neville quickly made up the distance between them. She refused to face him so he brought her back up against his chest and held her about her waist. He leaned down to place his chin on the top of her head. "Are you trying to tell me your marriage has never been consummated?"

"Shamefully, I must admit this is so," she whispered, hiding her face in her hands. "There must be something terribly wrong with me if I cannot tempt my husband to perform his duties in our marriage bed."

"Gwendolyn, there is nothing wrong with you," Neville chuckled, amused she would think she was undesirable.

She whirled around to face him with a frown. "Are you mocking me, Drayton? I will not stand for being the butt of some cruel joke, sir."

"I rather believe you will be one of the most exasperating women it has ever been my pleasure to encounter."

Her brow rose at his words. Her hands came to push against his chest but Neville continued to hold her close. "And just how many women do you plan to *meet* in your lifetime, Drayton?"

"Do not be cross with me, Gwendolyn. If it were up to me, you would be the last woman on earth who would ever own my heart," he whispered before once more capturing her lips in a kiss.

Her arms wrapped themselves around his neck and he pulled her even closer so she could have no doubt he wanted her more than he had ever wanted another woman. When he at last let her up for a breath of air, he could see in the depths of her eyes she was just as affected by their kiss.

"You are forgiven, Neville."

"You are most gracious, my lady," he smiled, placing his hand over his heart. "Never think, even in the smallest measure in that beautiful head of yours, that I do not want you or that you are undesirable. If Sandhurst is unable to perform his husbandly duties then there is something wrong with him and not you, my dear."

"You are easing my mind, Neville. Thank you."

"Besides, this could work to our advantage. If the marriage has not yet been consummated, than perhaps we can procure an annulment for you."

She gasped. "An annulment? I will be the laughing stock of Society, and seen as the woman who could not please her husband."

Neville's eyes narrowed. "You would rather stay married to him?"

A sound burst forth from her mouth. Part laugh, part snort, part outrage that he even voiced such a travesty out loud. "Are you mad? I despise the man and that feeling will never change even if I am stuck with him for the next twenty years."

"We will think of something, along with when we can arrange another meeting. I cannot in good conscience rely on your brother's good nature and discretion to continue meeting in his home."

"Brandon understands, even though I do not think there is another brother alive who would ever allow his sister to have an illicit encounter with another man beneath his very roof. Hartford would have a fit if he were to find out what we were all up to."

Neville took out his watch and noted the time.

"Worthington may be understanding but you are still his sister. I sincerely doubt he will continue to be so gracious, especially if you leave here appearing so beautifully disheveled."

"Oh, dear. I must look a fright," she declared.

"Nothing could be farther from the truth. Even your lips are rosy from our kisses."

"They are?" she asked breathlessly bringing her fingertips up to touch her lips.

"Yes, they are." Neville took her hand away before leaning forward to kiss her again. "You best fix your hair, Gwendolyn. Worthington will be here shortly to see you home."

"So soon?"

"Dinner can only last so long, my dear. There is no sense in giving Sandhurst reason to become suspicious you are doing anything more than having dinner with your brother."

"Yes, of course. I did not think of that. I am not accustomed to sneaking around and concocting lies to cover my whereabouts." Her voice trembled.

"That is because you are good at heart. I promise we will think of something to remedy our situation."

Neville pulled her into his arms one last time. One moment he was kissing her senseless, and the next he was watching her leave with her brother. Upon Worthington's return, they would need to think of a way to get Gwendolyn out of her loveless marriage. He wanted her to be happy. *He* wanted to be happy. His only solution to remedy his misery was to have Gwendolyn as his wife and be damned to what Society thought of them.

THIRTEEN

$\mathcal{B}$ ERNARD CONTINUED SIPPING his drink. "Report." He leaned back in his chair to peer at the man before him.

"There is not much to tell, your lordship. Lady Sandhurst arrived at her brother's house for the evening meal, as she told you, where she has remained."

"You did not see anyone else enter after she arrived?"

"No, my lord. When I saw Lord Brandon's carriage was being brought around, I assumed she would be returning home shortly and came here straight away to report to you as we agreed upon."

Bernard refilled his glass. "Next time, wait to see if anyone else leaves the household afterwards. You can report to me the next morning instead."

"As you wish, Lord Sandhurst."

Bernard waved the man away but not before handing him several coins. "That is all." He stood and began following the gentleman to the front door. "Hollis will see you out." Bernard nodded to his butler and made his way to the parlor to await his wife. A servant came to turn up the wicks to lighten the room but he dismissed them. He did not mind waiting in the near dark.

His wife entered the house a short time later and Bernard could have sworn her eyes looked brighter. "Ah, my loving wife returns to her husband."

Gwendolyn gave a started gasp and peered into the dimly lit room. Handing her wrap to Hollis, she came to the parlor and turned up the wick on one of the table lights. "You gave me such a start, my lord. Whatever are you doing here sitting in the dark?"

"Drinking and waiting for you."

"Are you drunk?" she inquired with a frown.

"Not yet, but I am getting there. What of it? At least I will not feel my sore foot."

"I do not know why you will not call for a doctor but brandy is not going to cure what ails you."

"My, are you not philosophical this evening." His words slurred together. Maybe he had had more to drink than he thought.

"I am no such thing. It is obvious your health is in need of a physician. If you do not care to heed my advice, than you have no one to blame but yourself for your misery. I am retiring. Good night, Lord Sandhurst."

Bernard stood, wavering on his feet, evidence he had indeed consumed a fair amount of spirits. "One moment, wife," he ordered and watched as she halted her progress, one hand still resting on the banister to the stairway.

She turned to face him with furrowed brows. "What is it, my lord? I am tired."

"I think it is past time we take our honeymoon trip."

"What?" Her eyes widened as another gasp escaped her parted lips. He watched her swallow several times.

"A wedding trip. We never took one. We should remedy the situation."

"We have been married six months, Lord Sandhurst. I hardly think a trip to celebrate our marriage is necessary at this point."

"Maybe a change of scenery will increase your ability to… please me." His eyes roamed up and down her body before he reached over to grasp her chin. "You do want to please me, do you not, dear wife?"

"Let me go, sir," she hissed at him through clenched lips.

"Ha! I will never let you go. You are my wife and therefore my chattel to do with as I please." He pulled her to him and managed to somehow place a sloppy kiss upon her mouth. She began pushing at him until he lost his grip upon her and she dashed up several steps before she turned around to face him. She wiped her mouth with the back of her hand as though disgusted with his touch.

"You have no right to touch me in your drunken condition," she seethed with eyes blazing in contempt.

"I have every right, wife, and will touch you anytime I wish it."

"You are inebriated and I am going to bed." Her angry stride took her up the remainder of the stairs until he heard her bedroom door shut a moment later.

Bernard went back to the parlor to retrieve his drink. Refilling the crystal, he slowly hobbled his way up to his chamber. Slamming the door, he fell upon the bed not even bothering to call for his servant to help him change out of his clothes. He passed out cold and dreamt of being a virile young man and satisfying his wife until she begged him for more. Come the morning, he would be just as impotent as he had been for all of his adult life, silently cursing every man who did not have the same damn problem.

FOURTEEN

$\mathcal{G}$ WENDOLYN FRANTICALLY FLICKED at the reins of her horse whilst she raced along the streets in the growing darkness of the night. She had had enough and could not stand being near her husband for an instant longer. His verbal insults had turned physical and he began slapping her around when she could not please him.

Had a fortnight really passed, since she had last seen Neville? She only knew the days, and nights, had seemed endless. In all that time, Bernard had barely let her out of his sight. He had even gone so far as to have her accompany him to his ship to see to the supplies being loaded for their journey. The thought of spending a month in the close quarters of a ship's cabin with him almost made her gag. How would she endure it?

If she had to spend another evening in his bed, she would scream and scream until her voice grew weak, and not care if he locked her away in some insane asylum. She would go mad if she had to stay within the same house with the man. He could not possibly have an inkling her heart went to another, but he seemed to sense something. Although she never let on that anything was different in their relationship, their marriage had changed for the worse the moment Neville Quinn swept into her life like a bright beacon offering her sanctuary. She had changed for the better, or so she thought.

Tears coursed down her cheeks at the unfairness of her miserable life. She silently cursed Bernard for making her do all those humiliating things night after night whilst he attempted to bed her. Luckily, every effort on his part was still to no avail. She remained a virgin and was thankful to at least still have that small part of herself as her own. She knew the law was on his side—she was his wife after all— but she needed to get away, at least for a time. She no longer cared what he would do to her upon her return home, nor what would happen to her reputation if she were to be found.

After his last failed attempt to consummate their marriage, he had shoved her onto the floor before he stormed out of the house, cursing her as always to the devil when he left. In her despair, she had come to a decision, however irrational it might be. Rare though it was for her to act on impulse—for she tended to run her life on a tight schedule—she had made her way to the stable to saddle her horse, refused the groom who would normally accompany her for a ride, and left the house with no clear destination in mind.

She would not go to Hartford, although she knew in her heart he would protect her with his last dying breath. No, if she went to Hartford, it would be as if she had forgiven him, and she was not sure she was ready to do so.

Logically she should have sought sanctuary at Brandon's, since he had already come to her aid more than once, had even aided her in privately seeing Neville. But instead of steering her horse toward the west side of town, she went in the opposite direction. She knew where *he* lived. That she was traveling in the direction of his townhouse was presumptuous on her part. To actually go there, unescorted, was unthinkable, but she did not care. She needed him as much as she needed air in her lungs. She had to see him, no matter the cost. She knew once he held her in those strong arms of his, she would know everything would be all right in the world. Neville would make everything better.

By the time she reached his townhouse, dusk had fallen. She barely reined in her horse before looking both ways to make sure she had not been followed. Jumping down, she tied the leather straps to the hitching post and raced up the walkway. Rapping on the door, she waited impatiently for it to open.

When the portal swung wide, she shielded her eyes from the light inside. Once her eyes adjusted to the brightness shining directly in her face, she expected to see a servant and not an unfamiliar young gentleman. He appeared to see nothing amiss in an unaccompanied lady knocking for entrance, but merely leaned upon the doorframe with an untied cravat, munching on an apple.

"I am sorry. I must have the wrong address," Gwendolyn confessed, starting to back down the pathway.

"Who are you looking for, my lady," he inquired looking past her into the darkness, probably for her escort. Her face flamed with heat, knowing she had none.

"I thought this was Lord Drayton's residence."

"You have the right place. I am Charles Quinn, Neville's younger brother," he announced opening the door, his smile edged with the curiosity he was too polite to express.

"A pleasure," she murmured not revealing her name. She had not known Neville had a brother, but they were still getting to know one another. She blanched at the thought she was standing here at the entryway, then flushed with embarrassment at her decision to call alone on an unmarried gentleman. What had she been thinking to do something so terribly reckless?

"Please do come in. Neville will take me to task if I allow a lady to stand outside in the cold," Mr. Quinn stated, grinning when a servant entered the foyer.

"Ah, Henry, punctual as usual." Mr. Quinn took another bite from his apple, before continuing. "Could you please see that the lady's horse is taken out back to the stable? I will also surmise Neville's guest is perhaps in need of a soothing pot of tea. Show her to the library, please. If you will excuse me, my lady, I shall go and get my brother."

"Thank you," Gwendolyn replied. Now that she could take a good look at Mr. Quinn, she could see for herself he was related to Neville. Only the color of their hair was different, for Mr. Quinn was blonde but she could still see hints of red.

"If you would follow me, madam," the servant said.

Gwendolyn hesitated and looked back at the dark street as though it offered some form of sanctuary. Such would not be found behind her in the still of the night but inside, where Neville would shortly join her.

She followed Henry, who opened the library door. The moment the door closed behind her, all her doubts returned full force. She had made a huge mistake in coming here. What would he think of her showing up on his doorstep? She had thought of no one but her own selfish need to be held by the man who had already stolen her heart. She had not given any thought to the consequences of her actions. Even so, despite her concerns, thoughts of her and Neville running away together continued to race through her mind.

The door opened and there he stood. His hair disheveled. His linen shirt opened, revealing a hint of bronzed hair upon his chest. She had obviously interrupted him preparing either to go out or to retire for the evening.

"Gwendolyn… whatever is wrong. Did he hurt you?"

She cared not what he thought of her. A sob escaped her lips even as she flew across the room to be enveloped in his arms. If she had to, she would spend a lifetime begging God to forgive her for her sins but she could not stay away from the man she loved. She rested her head upon his chest and could hear for herself his heartbeat, racing much like her own. Arms of steel wrapped around her and she knew without any doubt she wished to stay forever within his arms.

She lifted her head and he brushed her hair from her face. "Neville… let us run away together," the words left her lips before she could retract them.

"Gwendolyn, we—"

Her fingers twisted in the linen of his shirt. "I cannot go back to him, Neville. Please, I beg of you, do not send me home. I cannot stand him touching me another day longer." She had been trying to stay strong for so long, but it was useless. The flood of tears finally released from the dam she had erected to protect what was left of her heart. Sob after heart-wrenching sob consumed her until she was struggling to breathe.

"Calm down, my sweet," Neville whispered, ushering her to a sofa. He quickly went to a sideboard and poured a small draught of sherry. He sat down next to her, handing her the crystal for her to sip. "I would do anything within my power for you, Gwendolyn, but I do not know how running away together would solve anything. Such a course can only lead to further problems. The law—"

"I do not give a fig about the law," she shouted. She raised her hand to her forehead before taking a sip of her drink. "I thought you would understand, Drayton."

"I *do* understand. You are upset; I recognize how you must be feeling, but I cannot imagine Sandhurst will let you leave without attempting to find your whereabouts, my dear," Neville stated calmly. His hand brushed down her hair before pulling her closer. "I do not relish the thought of being tossed into a Tower of London cell for aiding you, although I would gladly do so if that is what you need from me."

"Then help me get to Berwyck. It is my family home near the Scottish border. The castle is a veritable fortress and I would be safe there. Hartford is not in residence at this time of year, so I know I will not have to deal with his censorship."

"I would think it would be only a matter of time before Sandhurst, and your brothers for that matter, will search for you in your family home," Neville reasoned, wiping a tear from her cheek.

Before he could withdraw his hand, she took hold of it, pressing her lips to his palm. "Then I will have a few days reprieve from the hell my life has become. Please tell me I can count on you to aid me, Neville. I do not relish traveling the length of England alone to reach Berwyck, but I will if I must."

"Running away never solves anything, Gwendolyn. No matter how we may wish differently, you will still be married to Sandhurst, and he has every right to drag you back to London if he so wishes," he warned, rubbing the back of his neck.

"Then he will have to drag me back here kicking and screaming," Gwendolyn vowed. "Will you come with me?"

"You know I will. I cannot let a woman travel the roads alone at night. Did you bring anything with you?"

"No, nothing but myself. I have clothing in my chambers at Berwyck so I will not be lacking in garments."

"Then let me have Jacob gather a few things for me and I will see that my carriage is brought around. We can leave immediately."

"Thank you, Neville."

"You are welcome." Neville kissed her on the forehead before heading to the door. "Are you sure you will not change your mind? Once we start on this course, there will be no turning back. The consequences will be heavy."

"I am certain. Please hurry, Neville."

He gave her a short bow before leaving the room. A housemaid came and brought her a cup of tea. Hoping to sooth her frayed nerves, she drank but it did not have the effect she was looking for. Her hands shook when she set the cup and saucer down on the table in front of her.

It was not until a short while later that she was finally able to relax. She was safe. Neville had made everything right in the world, at least for now. She was snuggled up against the warmth of Neville's body with his arm wrapped around her bringing her close. It was the first time in months that she slept soundly, with pleasant dreams of being loved by the very man who was even now watching her intently as she dozed.

FIFTEEN

EVILLE AND GWENDOLYN travelled all that
night, through the next day, and into the
following night, never stopping for longer than it took to
change horses. Gwendolyn was desperate to get to Berwyck
before Lord Sandhurst caught them, and Neville could not
help but think being caught on the road would go harder on
her than being found in her ancestral home.

In the late afternoon of the second day, they finally
arrived at Berwyck Castle. As she had mentioned, it was an
impressive estate with the keep sitting high above on a cliff
side, the ocean far below. He had been shown to a chamber
on the third floor of the keep and, once he was settled, he
went to find his lady.

Neville climbed the turret stairs after being told Lady
Sandhurst could be found on the battlement walls of the
keep. Once he was on the rooftop, he saw her near the outer
wall. He did not wish to disturb her solitude just yet and
instead hovered near the door in order to take in the

picturesque beauty—not the admittedly spectacular landscape, but Gwendolyn.

Her back was to him whilst she stared off into the distance. Her brown hair was left unbound and swirled around her from the ocean breeze. Her pale blue gown clung to her body like a second skin, and if he had not known better he would have once again sworn she was an angel from heaven or a medieval princess awaiting her knight to come to her rescue.

She must have somehow known he was near for she turned and smiled in his direction. She lifted her arm, beckoning him to join her. He began making his way towards her, up several more steps before carefully treading upon the narrow parapet. He did not know many women who would feel comfortable on the slight walkway.

Gwendolyn lifted her face and he leaned down to bestow a kiss upon her rosy lips. Her contented sigh of pleasure reached his ears, making his heart soar. "You were far away. Good thoughts, I hope," he asked watching her face light up with happiness.

"Yes, they were." She intertwined her fingers with his. "I was thinking of you."

"Were you now?" His brows rose in amusement.

She peered at him warily but her amusement was evident from the small crinkles of merriment near her eyes. "Tell me you are not one of those conceited men who requires flattery from his lady every day, are you, Drayton?"

He chuckled. "Surely you are not speaking of me, or are you, dearest Gwendolyn? I am deeply offended you could think of me thusly." He put his hand over his heart as though she had indeed wounded him.

Her sweet laughter bubbled forth like a fountain in

springtime and he was pleased he could make her laugh. "You cad, Drayton," she teased, before tugging upon his jacket. "Kiss me."

"You injure my manly pride and now you demand a kiss. Whatever am I to do with you, Gwendolyn?"

"I am certain you will think of something." Her arms wrapped around his neck and she pressed herself against him.

"You are going to test my ability to remain a gentleman if you continue your current course. You are treading dangerous waters, my lady," he warned mischievously.

"And I can see by that roughish grin upon your handsome face that you may not mind at all if you compromise my virtue."

He gulped as he sensed a part of him awakening to her gentle promptings. "Gwendolyn—" She reached up and placed her fingertips upon his lips, silencing his protest.

"Not now, Neville," she whispered moistening her lips with her tongue. "Let us enjoy the moment and worry about our troubles on the morrow. Kiss me," she demanded yet again.

His resolve broken, he pulled her to him in a firm embrace and lowered his head to give in to her request. He certainly had a weakness when it came to this lady. One word from her and he was more than content to do her bidding.

Neville deepened their kiss. Their bodies molded perfectly, one to the other. His hand moved down her backside and he urged her further into his own muscled body. There was no doubt she could sense what she had done to him. She did not seem to mind the intrusion to her maidenly sensibility for she followed his lead, her tongue warring with his.

Her moan was like the sweetest music to his ears. His heart raced that he was the one to evoke such an emotion from her. If he did not stop this now, he would be a doomed man for the rest of his days. This woman, who held on to him as if he alone could save her from her fate, had woven her way into his heart before he had even realized what was happening. He never wanted to leave her side again.

Neville reluctantly tore his lips from hers. "You, my dear, could tempt a saint to sin."

A small elusive smile lit her face. She knew exactly what she had done to him and was like a satisfied cat purring contently in his ear. "I know not of what you speak, my dearest Drayton."

He laughed and she joined in. It was so good to witness her defenses down and see her so happy. If only all their days could remain so. "We have had a long trip. The evening meal is ready for us in the Great Hall. Shall we dine?" he asked holding out his arm for her to take.

When they were making their way down the winding turret stairs, Gwendolyn would stop every dozen steps and ask him for another kiss. When she finally allowed them to gain entrance to the hall, she twirled around in the room.

"It feels so good to be home. This place is always so good for my soul."

"I am delighted I could bring you here then, Gwendolyn, especially to see you so content."

"I am perfectly content, Neville, whenever I am with you." Her eyes sparkled in delight whilst she watched him.

He escorted her to a table that had been set for them next to a roaring fire in the massive hearth. He could imagine days of old, when knights would fill the room eating their fill with minstrels playing afterwards as those same knights and their ladies danced the night away.

Dinner had never been more pleasant as they conversed and learned more about one another. As the evening waned, Neville regretted when he had to bid her good night. He had watched her drift down the passageway to find her chamber whilst he went to his own wondering if there would ever come a time when he would be able to claim Gwendolyn as his wife. Their future did not look very bright as he lay down on the mattress of his bed very much alone.

SIXTEEN

$\mathcal{W}$HEN SHE LEFT her chamber, Gwendolyn's heart beat at a rapid pace at what she was about to do. She made her way down the passageway on bare feet. Earlier, a maid had been waiting for her in her room to assist her with undressing. Once her corset and stays had been unlaced, and Gwendolyn had been able to at last take a deep breath, she dismissed her. She could manage the rest herself. She had sat in her room debating her next course of action for what seemed like hours, before she took hold of her courage and sealed her own fate.

Her nightclothes floated behind her in a trail of silk. She was resolved that she would not spend this night alone, nor remain a virgin any longer. She only prayed Neville would not reject her offer. She was not sure if her heart could bear the disappointment if he refused what she would willingly offer.

She came to his door and raised her hand to knock but hesitated in mid-air. What was she doing? Could she really go through with this? What would he think of her? Did his feelings for her run just as deep as her own? They had not, in truth, known each other for a long amount of time but she could not deny her invisible connection to Neville Quinn. Did he feel it too?

She bit her lip in indecision before she once more decided her fate. Gwendolyn knocked softly upon the door that barred her entrance to the one man she loved with all her heart. She pressed her ear to the wood wondering if he heard her, for she could not detect any noise coming from inside. Blasted castle with walls made of stone made discovering if he had heard her near to impossible. She knocked again and this time heard a mumbled response. She backed up against the far side of the passageway wall to await him.

The door swung open to reveal Neville in a long flowing robe that he was still in the process of tying at his waist. "Is something wrong?" he asked whilst his eyes raked over her like a gentle caress. She shivered with anticipation of what this night would bring, for her body's natural reaction to seeing him standing there had nothing to do with being cold.

"N-no. There is nothing wrong. In f-fact, everything is p-perfectly... right." Was that her voice sounding so shaky and insecure? Could she really go through with this insane idea of hers?

His brows drew together. "Then what are you doing standing there in a drafty corridor at this hour?"

Yes, I can, she answered herself before pushing off the wall to walk past Neville to enter his chamber. She had always loved this room, for it had been reserved for the castle's captain of the guard in years long since passed. How fitting was it that she had ensured he would make use of this room during their stay? He certainly had come to her rescue and saved her from the sorry state of her life, even though her rescue was only a temporary one.

She made her way to stand before the fire for she knew the light would outline her body beneath her nightclothes. How many times had Bernard asked her to stand thusly in the hopes that the image would arouse him? She shook any further thoughts of her husband from her mind. This night belonged to herself and Neville.

"Gwendolyn…" His voice, his deep husky tone, reached down to invisibly touch the very deepest recesses of her soul.

She turned to face him and there could be no doubt that he desired her, for his passion was clearly etched upon his handsome features as though he had spoken the words aloud.

"Yes, Neville?" she asked in a seductive whisper.

"What are you doing here?"

A small laugh burst forth from her lips making Gwendolyn wonder when she had felt this content. The fact that some distant memory did not flash through her mind was a testament to how miserable her life had been since her marriage. "I would think the reason would be perfectly obvious, darling," she continued and proceeded to give her head a shake. Her long flowing curls swayed back and forth as the tresses settled back into place. She smiled, knowing she had Neville's complete attention.

"You cannot mean…"

She walked back across the room only to go past him and shut the door. She slid the bolt into place to ensure their privacy. "Of course I do," she replied, finishing his thoughts for him.

She made her way around him, her fingertips skimming lightly over his tense body that she wished was not covered in his robe. She finally faced him. She had never seen him look nervous before, which only endeared him all the more to her heart. She had clearly roused him from his slumber, since his auburn hair was sticking up in several places. She wished she could reach the strands to put them back into place. She felt so small standing next to him, for he was so tall, and for the first time in her life she felt like a desirable woman.

She reached up to push his robe aside. Her hands came to rest upon the warmth of his bare furred chest and she almost sighed in pleasure to at last be touching him. He, on the other hand, had his arms at his sides with his fists clenched whilst apparently attempting to remain a gentleman. Such an effort was hardly necessary.

"Gwendolyn, you cannot expect me to deflower you here in your brother's home of all places." He spoke the obvious with a firm pitch of resolve to remain chivalrous. "I am only a mere mortal man and not carved from stone to resist your advances for long."

"Then do not resist, Neville."

"One of us has to remain the voice of reason."

"Why? This is all really very simple. I want you to make love to me." She wantonly pressed herself up against him and heard his indrawn breath. She laughed. "I can also see for myself you want me too."

"Of course I want you. I would need to be insane not to want you for the rest of my days." He groaned aloud when she pressed herself once more against him.

She reached up to trace his lips before making her way

back towards the hearth. When she turned to face him, she let her robe fall to the floor in a puddle of silken linen.

"Give me this night, Neville. I know I will have no choice but to go back to him once he finds me, but please, let me have this one night to always remember. One night with you that will be burned into my memory, telling me how life could have been if only our situation was different."

She reached up and let her nightgown slowly fall to the floor. There was certainly no turning back, now that she stood naked before him.

"Gwendolyn," he choked out. His eyes smoldered whilst he caressed every inch of her body with those mesmerizing hazel eyes.

"One night, Neville. That is all I ask of you, for I know I cannot ask for more."

He moved so quickly he reminded her of a tiger pouncing upon its prey. She did not mind in the least when he captured her in the strength of his arms and carried her to his bed. She moved to the center and when he tore the robe from his body her breath left her.

He was magnificent. She had known he would be. Perfectly formed in every way. The bulging muscles of his arms were well molded, but she already knew this. He had already proven he had more than enough strength, since he had been capable of carrying her several furlongs with ease. The hard-ridged muscles of his chest and stomach reminded her of a finely sculpted piece of art. Her fingers tingled. She wanted to skim her hands over his entire body to reassure herself that he was real and not just some figment of her imagination. Her eyes moved lower and she smiled. Clearly she had no problem arousing the man standing before her.

And then Gwendolyn had no further time for thoughts

about Neville's appearance for he joined her in his bed. He seemed in no hurry to take his pleasure but instead he raised her hand to his lips and kissed it.

"I have waited a lifetime to find you, sweet Gwendolyn," he whispered, his voice hoarse as though he held back the passion he had been keeping in check.

She reached up to caress his cheek. "And I you, my dearest Neville."

"Tonight belongs to us."

"Yes. Tonight I belong only to you." Her hand wrapped around his neck and he leaned down to put a gentle kiss upon her lips. "Love me, Neville."

"I already do, my sweet."

She smiled in delight at his declaration. "Then make me forget everything else but you."

As Neville brought her closer into his arms and began to kiss her, Gwendolyn sighed in pleasure. Just experiencing the heat of his naked body pressed up against her own caused Gwendolyn's heart to rejoice with her need to be with this man. *So, this was how loving someone was supposed to be*, she thought before Neville made her forget anything else but how to *feel*. For the first time in her life, Gwendolyn knew what it was like to be cherished by a man she loved.

Far into the night they loved one another and when Neville at last made them one, Gwendolyn's cry of pain was smothered with another one of his tantalizing kisses that left her dizzy. Yet that was nothing compared to when they began to move in a rhythm known to lovers from the beginning of time itself. And when she found her release for the very first time at the height of their lovemaking, she surely must have soared up to the heavens with this man who had taken flight with her. As she returned back down to earth and snuggled into the warmth of Neville's arms, she knew she would never be the same ever again.

SEVENTEEN

$\mathcal{B}$ ERNARD WAS JUST finishing his breakfast when Hollis entered. "Why are you disturbing me," he asked, his mouth full of the last of his eggs.

"My apologies, your lordship, but there is a Mr. Smith to see you, sir. He stated the matter was of some urgency and you would wish to see him."

"Do not keep the man waiting, Hollis. Bring him in at once," he snapped.

Bernard eyed the sideboard and gave into his stomach's rumble telling him he was still hungry. He motioned for a servant to fill his plate again. When the dish was put before him, he began eating his fill for a second time. Or was this his third helping? No matter, he ate until *Mr. Smith* entered. A convenient name that, *Smith*. Bernard waved the man in.

"Care for breakfast, Mr. Smith?" Bernard muttered with his mouth full. "Plenty here."

"No thank you, Lord Sandhurst. I have already eaten."

"You may leave us," he said dismissing the nearby

servant. "Take a seat then, *Mr. Smith*." He chuckled knowing the man before him was hiding his identity, not that this mattered in his household. Bernard knew his servants were loyal to him.

Smith took a seat half way down the long table. "I have something of a delicate nature to report, sir."

Bernard looked up from his meal to glare at the man. Setting his fork down, he wiped his mouth with a linen napkin then leaned back into his chair. Resting his hands on his protruding stomach, he belched. "Well, get on with it man. Tell me what you have found out about my wife."

"She's gone north, your lordship."

"North? Where north?"

"To her family's estate at the Scottish border. To Berwyck, sir." The man ran his finger across the neck of his cravat as if the cloth was too tight.

"And what else? I can tell you have more to report than just the news of my wife traveling to Berwyck."

"She did not go alone."

Heat flooded Bernard's face. He knew this was going to happen yet again. This was the cost of taking another woman to wife who was too beautiful and young for her own damn good, or his. He should have never signed the marriage contract years ago with the previous Duke of Hartford, nor should he have agreed with the man's son to honor the contract. At the time, the agreement had seemed like a worthy exchange. The previous Duke's bet was settled in Bernard's favor. The current Duke avoided a public scandal over being insolvent and unable to meet his financial obligations. Bernard won a beautiful woman as his wife. The situation benefited everyone, or so he had surmised at the time.

"Did she travel with one of her brothers?" Bernard asked through clenched lips, clinging to one last bit of hope.

"I am afraid not, my lord."

"Then tell me the blackguard's name!" The candlesticks shook when he slammed his fists onto the table.

"The Earl of Drayton."

Shame coursed through Bernard. He was being deceived and betrayed by yet another wife. That Drayton actually had the gall to be found in Bernard's own home, set his temper flaring even higher. How long had this been going on beneath his very nose? He thought he had been keeping Gwendolyn well within sights, but apparently she was smarter than he thought. Yes, and braver, given that the wench actually had the nerve to travel without his knowledge.

"Hollis," Bernard shouted. He did not have to wait long for his man to stand at the doorway, his face completely expressionless. "Have my clothes packed and the carriage brought around. I am leaving for Berwyck immediately."

"I shall take my leave, your lordship." Mr. Smith rose from the table and began to depart.

"Just where the devil do you think you are going?"

"I assumed we had concluded our business, sir."

Bernard peered at the man whilst a plan suddenly formed inside his head. "Far from it, Mr. Smith. I am still in need of your services."

Bernard made his way to his study to pen a note to his ship's captain. As soon as he collected Gwendolyn, he would make for the vessel. Maybe some time away from London would allow the chit to remember she was a married woman with a husband who would not let her out of his sight again.

EIGHTEEN

*T*HERE WAS NOTHING like spending a relaxing day on the beach with a beautiful woman at your side. Neville lay propped up on one elbow and watched Gwendolyn. Her hair blew in disarray from the ocean's breeze but what held him captivated was the peaceful look of contentment upon her lovely face. He had never seen her look so happy, and he was more than content himself knowing he was the cause. Had it really been two days since that glorious night when they had made love far into the early morning hours? They had not been apart since.

He knew their situation would not last long. It was only a matter of time before he would need to see her home. Or, worse yet, they came for her themselves, *they* being either her brothers or her husband. No matter who came to retrieve her, it would not bode well for their situation. Neville dreaded letting her go, but how could he not, when she was married to another man?

Gwendolyn put the remains of their luncheon into the

basket and smoothed the blanket where it had become tangled at their feet. Reaching for her bonnet, she began to tie the ribbon beneath her chin. It was hard for Neville to watch the transition. Once her task was completed, the carefree woman of but a moment before was replaced with the demure daughter of a duke that she was, reminding him of all the barriers between them. Their gazes met and she gave him a small hesitant smile. Neville could tell that she, too, was thinking their time together was almost at an end.

Before he thought better of it, he gathered her in his arms and crushed his mouth to hers. It was a possessive kiss. One that would surely be engraved upon each of their souls so they remembered that, no matter what, they would somehow be together again.

They pulled apart and a sob escaped her whilst she turned away from him to collect herself. "Neville… I cannot stand the thought of leaving you, although I know I must. I will treasure these past few days until we can somehow be together again."

Neville pulled her to her feet and held her. She fit in his arms as if she were made to be there as no other had ever before. "Gwendolyn, I promise you we will be together some day. I do not know when or how, but no other will ever lay claim upon my heart but you." His heartfelt declaration brought more tears to her eyes that he wiped away.

"I cannot ask you to wait for me, Drayton. That would be too selfish on my part. You must go on and live your life."

"You *are* my life and I care not how long I must wait for you. Do you actually think I could be with another after what we have shared?"

"You are a handsome man with needs, Drayton," she declared with firm lips. "Even I know I cannot ask you to remain celibate waiting God only knows how long for my husband to die of old age."

"I will wait an entire lifetime for you if I must, my sweet Gwendolyn. You *are* my life and I will have no other but you," he repeated. He lifted her hand to his lips and brought her close.

"Neville…"

"We will find a way, my love."

He kissed her again to seal his vow before intertwining his fingers with hers as they began to stroll back to the castle along the strand. Berwyck was an impressive sight sitting high upon the cliff and he could understand why she felt safe here. His own estate near the south of England may not have been as large as this stronghold, but his castle was just as secure.

Gwendolyn's laugh brought him out of his musings. "Do you like Berwyck, as well, Neville?"

"Of course. I can see why you wished to come here." He lifted her hand to his lips whilst they continued walking.

"Legends say that centuries ago, some traveled through time to meet their knights or ladies here on this very beach, or other places nearby," her eyes twinkled with merriment whilst she watched him.

Neville laughed. "I suppose your mother used to tell you such fanciful stories as she tucked you into bed as a child."

"And my grandmother," she answered, stopping to gaze off into the distance. "Both women were truly romantic at heart and loved their husbands very much. My father was a stern man and may have arranged my marriage to a man I detest, but I still loved him all the same." She shook her head coming out of her thoughts. "If only it were true…"

"Such stories are for children, my love, but I am glad you have pleasant memories of your grandmother to cherish."

"As do I. The story she used to tell me of a ghost keeping watch over the castle and its inhabitants I could do without. But she was an incredible woman. She would have liked you."

"I am glad you think so, despite the circumstances in which we find ourselves currently in."

"I am afraid she would not have approved of me dishonoring my marriage vows," Gwendolyn replied with downcast eyes, "no matter how much she loved me."

"I have no regrets, my love."

She looked up at him and gave him another small smile. "Nor do I," she whispered.

They continued towards the castle. Gwendolyn stopped every now and then to point out various places of interest from her childhood or where stories of old supposedly took place. She told of an escape tunnel that at one time led from the floor housing the family members of the castle down to the strand, but it had collapsed ages ago.

He enjoyed listening to her stories of her ancestors, as well as once more seeing the happy woman he had come to love. Yes… love her he did, despite knowing he should not.

They at last crossed the wooden bridge and dry moat leading into the outer bailey of the keep. Gwendolyn's laugher died on her lips whilst her face suddenly fell. Neville turned to see what she stared at. He placed his hand on her shoulder and she turned into his embrace with a sob.

There could be no mistaking the ducal emblem emblazoned upon the resplendent coach parked near the stables. The team of horses had already been unhitched, giving evidence Hartford had been inside for some time.

Neville wiped her tears and gave her one last kiss before they began to make their way to the keep. Their time together was at an end. It was time to pay for their reckless indiscretion.

NINETEEN

$\mathcal{G}$ WENDOLYN CLUTCHED AT Neville's arm as though he was the only person capable of supporting her. They stood together in Hartford's study. Her brother paced back and forth before the hearth, his cravat untied, his hair a mess. For the first time Gwendolyn could remember since her brother had inherited the title from their father, he was not immaculately attired and seemingly in control.

Brandon sat in a chair with a brandy in one hand, the other holding his head. One look into his eyes and she could see he was sorry for being here with Hartford, and not just for the trouble he had undoubtedly had in explaining his part in this whole sorry situation of theirs. She knew her younger brother well. It was not hard to figure out that he had planned hers and Neville's encounter in the park. Yet, she was thankful for his interference and would tell him directly just as soon as the opportunity presented itself.

She waited for Hartford's anger to erupt. She did not have long to wait.

"Damn it, Gwendolyn. What the hell were you thinking? Brandon and I were sick with worry not knowing your whereabouts. And the fright you have given mother! How could you worry her like that?" Hartford shook his head in disgust before striding swiftly to his desk to grab an empty crystal glass. He thrust the cup toward his brother who took the nearby decanter and filled alcohol to the rim.

She watched Hartford drink part of his brandy and slam the glass down onto the mantle of the fireplace before she answered. "I am not sorry," she declared with a lift of her chin.

Neville stepped forward. "Hartford, if we can speak privately I—"

Hartford crossed the distance of the room faster than Gwendolyn thought possible. He grabbed at Neville's neck cloth bringing them nose to nose. "How dare you compromise my sister and in my own bloody house," he roared, his face turning an unsightly shade of red.

"Edmond, no!" Gwendolyn screamed, trying to put herself between the two men but to no avail.

Neville put up his hands. "I will not fight you, Your Grace."

"The hell you will not. I demand satisfaction for what you have done to my sister." Edmond took a firmer hold on Neville's neck cloth, giving him a shake, before Brandon came to pull the two apart.

"Leave him be, Edmond. Whatever has happened between them cannot be undone," Brandon urged, filling another glass and offering the drink to Neville.

Edmond turned on Brandon, his voice arctic cold. "Why do I have the distinct feeling in my gut that you know what has been going on with these two?"

Brandon shrugged. "She was unhappy. I could see for myself Drayton could change that. If you but care to get your head out of your ass, you would see for yourself they love one another."

"But she is already married!" Edmond bellowed.

"And whose fault is that?" Gwendolyn hissed. "I will never love Sandhurst." Standing between her two brothers, she nodded to Brandon who returned to his chair by the fire. She looked over her shoulder to Neville, who came to stand next to her and she linked her arm with his.

Edmond met her glare with one of his own, then his eyes softened and he sat back down and reached for his drink. In a much milder tone, he said, "I swear you will be the death of me, Gwendolyn Marie. Do you know what your disappearance did to us when we found you missing? Anything could have happened to you in London."

"Neville kept me safe."

Brandon raised his glass. "And for that we are thankful, are we not Edmond?"

Edmond's brow rose as he stared at them before he gave a heavy sigh. "Yes, I will admit I am grateful, although I say so under major protest."

"I understand, Hartford." Neville gave a brief nod, pulling Gwendolyn closer. "If I could and it was my right, I would always ensure that your sister was safe."

Edmond ran his hand across the back of his neck in frustration. "You two have put me in a difficult situation. I adhered to the wishes of our father to see you married to Sandhurst. I may not have said it aloud, but I did not like seeing my beloved sister married to a man who was old enough to be her father but he swore he would do all in his power to make you happy. And what is done is done. You *are* married to Sandhurst and the law will be on his side. You must return to him, Gwendolyn."

"I know," Gwendolyn whispered.

Edmond held out a sheet of parchment. "You should read this, Gwen."

Gwendolyn detached herself from Neville to take the paper from her brother. As she read, her eyes widened before she covered her mouth in shock and fell into a nearby chair. "My word. I had no idea he has been following me."

Neville came to stand next to her and read the missive for himself over her shoulder. "Then he knows." He downed his drink in a single gulp.

Edmond stood, reaching for the decanter for brandy to refill Neville's glass. "Yes, as I have been following him. I may not have been able to release Gwendolyn from the commitment made by our father, given her original agreement, but that does not mean I have not been keeping a close eye on him."

"He will not be kind to me when I have to return," Gwendolyn stated. She began to shake in fear of what her future held at the hands of her husband.

"Tell them, Gwendolyn," Neville urged.

She turned her eyes upward to Neville. She may have confessed her husband's problem to the man who held her heart, but she could not imagine sharing such embarrassing intimacies with her brothers. "I cannot." She stood, and buried her face in Neville's chest whilst his arms wrapped around her.

Brandon leaned forward in his chair. "Tell us what you know. Perhaps whatever Gwen is not telling us can get her out of this marriage."

Neville gave her a kiss on her forehead and tightened his arms around her. "Sandhurst is impotent. Gwendolyn was a virgin when we… err… when we…"

Edmond cleared his throat. "I get the picture. No need for further explanations."

Gwendolyn turned to face her brother. "Edmond, I need you to get me an annulment."

"An annulment? That takes time, Gwen," Edmond answered running his hand through his hair. "Besides, it appears you and Drayton have removed the evidence of your *situation*, so there will be no case if an examination is requested."

Gwendolyn blushed still deeper and hid her face in Neville's chest once more.

Brandon laughed. "Is that not a hoot? The old man could not even consummate his marriage. What luck!"

"Luck?" Gwendolyn shrieked, wagging her finger at Brandon. "You have no idea what that lecherous old man has me do each time he thinks he is capable of finally bedding me. The thought of going back to that vile excuse for a human being makes my stomach churn in disgust."

Neville pulled her back into his arms. "Easy now, love. Brandon does not mean to upset you."

Gwendolyn patted his arm before again leaving his embrace, returning her gaze to her older brother. "Please pull whatever strings you can to get me out of this horrible marriage, Edmond. I do not give a fig what society thinks of me, even if they regard me as nothing but a common trollop. I have no issue going into seclusion if necessary. In time they will forget there was any scandal whatsoever associated with my name."

Neville took her hand and bowed over it. "Once you are

free of him, then I hope you would honor me by becoming my wife. With your brother's permission, of course."

She cupped his cheek smiling into his hazel eyes. "Nothing would make me happier than to accept your proposal as soon as I am able."

Gwendolyn was brought back to reality when Edmond cleared his throat to gain their attention.

"I hate to break this up, but I will have you know that Sandhurst will be here shortly. You have another day together at the most. You had better make the best of it," Edmond grumbled, "not that I am approving of you further compromising my sister, Drayton."

Brandon held back a laugh. "Let it go, Edmond. They are in love. Let them be happy for the little amount of time they have left together."

Edmond turned blazing eyes upon his brother. "You and I, however, are not finished with this discussion. You always were too easy going and unconventional. How you could play a part in this fiasco is beyond my comprehension. She is your sister, for God sake!" Edmond's fuming caused Brandon to once more stifle a laugh.

"Please be easy on him, Edmond," Gwendolyn murmured. "I will be forever grateful to our younger brother for seeing how miserable I was and assisting me with an opportunity I would never have dared on my own." Gwendolyn crossed to Brandon and gave him a hug. She then made her way to Edmond. She waited only a moment before she hurled herself into his arms. Today's discussion had begun to heal the hurt she had felt for his apparent betrayal when he insisted she honor her commitment to her marriage with Bernard. He kissed her cheek.

"I will do all in my power to see your marriage dissolved,

Gwen," he vowed, and she had no reason to doubt he would do just that.

"Thank you, Edmond," she whispered before grabbing Neville's hand and rushing from the room.

If they had only one more day together, she would take her brother's advice and make the most of their time. Racing down the passageway, they reached the door to her bedroom. Gwendolyn smiled, pulled Neville inside, and watched him lock the door to shut out the world. He wasted no time taking her into his arms and she gave a contented sigh, knowing this was where she truly belonged.

TWENTY

NEVILLE PUSHED BACK the heavy tresses of Gwendolyn's hair that had fallen about them. They were like a heavenly veil of dark silk. Staring up into her passion-filled brown eyes, he wondered where this remarkable woman had been all his life. She leaned down and kissed him before he rolled her from her position on top of him. She snuggled into his side placing her hand over his heart.

"I do not know how I will keep up with you, my dear," he laughed with a smirk. "I need a moment, or perhaps two, in order to recover from our last exertion."

Gwendolyn reached down between them to grasp his already rising manhood. "You keep up... just fine, Drayton," she murmured seductively before she began nibbling on his earlobe.

"If I had not been the man to take your maidenhead, I would have sworn you were more experienced in making love than a virgin. You catch on quickly to what arouses me, my love."

"I have a good teacher." She laid her head back down upon his chest whilst her fingertips began tracing circles upon his stomach.

He caught her hand when it began to move lower and raised it to his lips. "A short reprieve, Gwendolyn. We should talk."

She flounced backwards onto her pillow. "I would rather do other more pleasurable things with our morning," she pouted.

He leaned upon one elbow to study her. "As would I, but the sun rises and the new day will bring about our unfortunate separation."

She scowled at him. "Why do you wish to ruin a perfectly fine morning talking about such unpleasantries, Drayton?"

Neville gave her sulking lips a quick kiss. "Because we must, my dearest."

"Very well," she muttered before rising from the bed and making her way across the room.

He watched her, fascinated with her swaying hips, the curve of her waist, the sleekness of her bared back beneath her glorious hair as it swayed back and forth. He admired how her tresses fell back into place after she lifted them out of the way while donning a robe.

Sitting down into a chair near the hearth, she extended one of her finely-shaped legs as though to examine its length before crossing one on top of the other and giving him a come-hither look. That she did not bother to cover her legs with the robe only made him want to peel the remainder of the fabric from her most delectable body. If he did not know better, he would have sworn she had performed such an act of seduction many times before. She was a born natural and he was captivated completely by the charms with which she teased him.

"What did you wish to speak about, Neville," she purred contently, knowing full well it would take every ounce of restraint on his part not to carry her back to the bed. He inwardly smiled, seeing her ploy, but two could play this game of hers.

He threw back the coverings of the bed and strolled slowly towards her. Her eyes glazed over and she licked her lips. Her gaze followed down the length of his body and he stopped his progress just to watch *her* watching *him*. Everything showed in her face. If he ever had a moment's doubt this woman wanted him, then they were hastily driven away in that instant.

"Gwendolyn." Her name whispered in the silence of the room shook her from her musings for she suddenly met his gaze with a becoming blush to be caught staring so openly at him. Not that he had given her any choice, standing there naked.

"Y-yes, Neville?" That delectable tongue peeked out of her most tempting mouth to moisten her lips yet again.

"You were staring, my sweet."

"I-I was?"

He chuckled. "Come here, Gwendolyn."

She moved so quickly that Neville suddenly had his arms full with a woman who molded herself to his body as though she were attaching herself to his skin.

"Hold me, Neville."

"I have you, Gwendolyn," he murmured into her hair as he tightened his arms around her waist.

"And never let me go," she continued in a rush.

He sighed. "If only it were that easy." She shuddered in

his arms. The feel of her shaking in his embrace broke his heart, knowing the cause. She would soon be with her husband and no longer with him.

"You will not forget me?" she asked, wrapping her arms tighter around his waist.

"How could I ever forget the lady who has stolen my heart," Neville remarked honestly.

"I have?"

There was so much doubt in her voice that he leaned down and kissed her. Not a possessive demanding kiss such as those they had shared during the midnight hours but a gentle one. A promise. A vow that somewhere in time they would one day be together again.

He broke their kiss and cupped her face with both his hands "I love you, Gwendolyn. For all time, I will love only you."

A sob escaped her. "Oh, Neville, I love you too."

Neville wrapped the crying woman in his arms. There was nothing he could do to ease her suffering except hold her. When her sniffling subsided, Gwendolyn attempted a small smile that nonetheless still left her lovely face drenched in sorrow. She left his arms and went to a table and began fumbling with the contents of a box.

"I know it is here somewhere," she stated and he watched as she pulled out various pieces of combs for her hair and set them on the table. "Ah, here it is."

The smile had spread to her eyes when she made her way back to his side and held out a small pendant.

"I should be the one giving you gifts, my dear, not the other way around," Neville protested.

Gwendolyn took his hand and placed the brass object in his palm. "I want you to have this. Go ahead. Turn it over."

Neville did as she bid and was pleased to see a miniature portrait of Gwendolyn staring back at him. She appeared younger by several years than she was now. She wore a light green dress with ermine trim. Her hair was swept up away from her face with one pleasing long length falling over her left shoulder. Her cheeks were blushed pink as she stared back at him with soft brown eyes. "I will treasure this, Gwendolyn, until we are reunited."

"Now you have something to remember me by. My father had it painted when I was about sixteen."

"Perhaps you should keep it then, dearest, as a remembrance of your sire."

She closed his fingers around the miniature portrait, "Please," she whispered in a hopeful plea, "I want you to have it."

"Then I shall cherish such a precious gift," he murmured pulling her once more into his arms.

The unmistakable sound of an approaching carriage broke them quickly apart. Gwendolyn ran to the window. She turned back towards him and rushed back to his side. "He is here," she cried out. "Kiss me, Neville."

He crushed her into his embrace, gladly giving in to her demand. One moment she was in his arms and the next he was hastily gathering his clothes. With one hand on the doorknob, he stole one more look at Gwendolyn who appeared to be struggling to catch her breath. She never looked lovelier.

"Be strong, Gwendolyn. We *will* be together again soon. I promise," Neville vowed before rushing from her room.

Neville had no more than gained entrance to his own chamber before he heard Sandhurst bellowing from far below, demanding to see his wife.

TWENTY-ONE

$\mathcal{G}$WENDOLYN'S FEET WERE as heavy as the walls of the fortress of Berwyck that had kept her safe for but a short while. Her heart was weighed down by what lay before her. As she descended the turret stairs of the keep, there could be no mistake in her husband's mood considering his bellow of outrage echoing in the air.

"By God, I swear I shall tear down this keep stone by stone with my bare hands if you do not produce my wife and the scoundrel who abducted her. I demand satisfaction from the misbegotten cur," he shouted and Gwendolyn could imagine her husband waving his fist in the air to get his point across.

She entered the Great Hall and made her way towards the gentlemen who stood at the hearth. "I am here, Lord Sandhurst. There is no need to voice idle threats that shall not be carried out, especially since I was hardly taken against my will." Gwendolyn made her declaration with a confident air and a lift of her chin.

Edmond stepped forward to bring her closer to his side. "Nor shall you threaten me within my own home, or did you forget to whom you are speaking?" The glare he tossed Sandhurst would have frozen a lake on the spot. Gwendolyn hid her smirk of satisfaction seeing her husband receive the full force of the ducal stare only Edmond could pull off with ease.

"M-my apologies, Your Grace. S-surely you must understand my c-concern for my w-wife?" Bernard stammered. He pulled a linen from his coat and began wiping the perspiration from his brow.

Brandon stepped forward to put his arm around his sister. The three stood together as a united front before the cowering man. "As you can see, Gwendolyn is perfectly safe."

"Yes… well… thank goodness for that."

Sandhurst's gaze traveled to study her from head to toe. She could in no way misinterpret the brief flicker of fury that flashed in his eyes before he masked his face with an insipid smile of mild disdain. His expression was anything but friendly and served as a forewarning of what was in store for her once they were alone. He would not be gentle, not when he knew another man had had his wife.

"Lord Sandhurst—" Gwendolyn began, only to clamp her lips shut when Bernard thrust out his hand to her. The gesture may appear as a kind invitation, but she knew better. Knowing she had no other recourse than to go with the man who, for now, held claim to her, she placed her warm fingers in his cold ones. She forced down a shudder at his touch.

"We must talk, Lady Sandhurst," he cajoled, bringing her fingertips up to his lips. "In private, I should think. We have much to discuss."

"But…" her voice trailed off. She had no idea of what would sway the man and make him listen to her objections. She stifled the urged to wipe her fingers where Sandhurst had left his wet mark on her, almost as a reminder that she belonged to him. Gwendolyn turned fearful eyes towards her brothers. They both held the same grim expression knowing they were powerless to deny the man his right to take her.

Nonetheless, Edmond tried. "I do not deny you the right to speak with my sister," he said, "but I consider it best she remain with her family for a short visit. I am sure you would not wish to deny me."

Gwendolyn was grateful, but she could tell from the brutal squeeze on her hand that Sandhurst had no intention of agreeing. The pleasantness of his answer was belied by the fury in his eyes.

"Very well, Your Grace. Lady Sandhurst, since the morning is such a beautiful day, let us take a stroll outside, just the two of us." He brought her closer, putting his arms about her waist and leaning to kiss her cheek. "How I have missed you, my dear sweet wife. Please excuse us, Your Grace. Worthington."

Sandhurst bowed, before pulling Gwendolyn through the length of the Great Hall and out the doors of the keep. The sound of the door closing caused her to flinch. It was as if she had just lost not only the connection to her brothers but to Neville as well. Was he even now watching them from one of the windows upstairs? She dared not take a glance in that direction.

"Lord Sandhurst," she began only to gasp as her arm was yanked hard. They halted their stride and Sandhurst leaned down until they were nose to nose.

"Not. One. Word. From. You. Our discussion will be held away from this castle so it remains private and not overheard by either your brothers or your... lover." The last word was hissed in anger.

Any further thoughts of protest were quickly dashed as they made their way through the inner and outer baileys. The barbican gate was opened, the portcullis raised high. How she could have wished both had remained lowered so no one, not even Sandhurst, could have entered.

He continued tugging at her arm whilst they crossed the drawbridge. The silence was deafening and she could take it no longer. "Where are we going?" Her frustrated tone had no effect, for Sandhurst just continued his frantic pace.

"You shall soon see." His smug look of satisfaction warned Gwendolyn to be leery. Yet, what could she do other than to obey him?

They continued their brisk pace through the village. Gwendolyn was unsure what they were running from or to, and had had no idea a man the size of her husband could move so fast. Yet he had no issue keeping up his hurried stride; his swift pace made it apparent his foot was not bothering today.

It was not until they made their way into the forest that he whirled upon her like a vicious snake intent on capturing its prey to squeeze the life from it whilst it coiled its form around its victim. He backed her up against a large oak, the bark abrasive on the delicate skin of her back. Gwendolyn's breath caught to see the fury Sandhurst had been holding in check. She had never seen him look so enraged before, although he had every right to be. She was not prepared for the slap that cracked like thunder and felt as hot as scorching fire, whilst his hand left its mark upon her cheek. Her head bounced back upon the tree whilst her vision reeled out of focus.

"You bloody whore from hell! You dare to make me a cuckold by sneaking away with another man?" His eyes bulged whilst spittle escaped from his pudgy lips in his tirade. His hand went to her throat and squeezed. "The first Lady Sandhurst thought she could get away with that stunt, but I will be damned if I will stand for having another adulterous wife in my life," he screamed out, his voice echoing in the forest.

Air. She needed air as he continued to choke her, his tight grip crushing her wind pipe. She clawed at his hands, but to no avail. Black spots started to form before her eyes until the sound of a male voice barely penetrated her head.

"Lord Sandhurst, cease," a voice shouted.

Another came to pry Sandhurst's fingers from her neck and, at last, he released her. Gwendolyn fell to the ground on her hands and knees, desperately gasping for air.

"How dare you touch me? Unhand me, Smith," Sandhurst yelled. "How I deal with my wife is none of your business. I pay you a handsome salary so remember you are under my employ. You will obey me, as will my *dear* wife," he sneered.

"Of course, my lord," Smith replied, before he continued, "However, I doubt the Duke of Hartford would take kindly to you abusing his sister, no matter that she is your wife."

Gwendolyn watched through teary eyes when the stranger finally let her husband go and Sandhurst began adjusting his clothing.

"Is everything ready?" Sandhurst asked, calm as though

he had not been attempting to take his wife's life but moments before. He tossed her what she could only term an evil grin. What ploy was he concocting behind the façade of his overly-friendly tone? Whatever it was, she had no way to prevent him.

"Yes, sir, just as you instructed. The horses are waiting just at the end of the forest."

"H-horses?" Gwendolyn managed to croak out.

Sandhurst moved like a far younger man and yanked her to her feet. She took a quick peek at the man he called Smith, hoping he might come to her rescue again. But nothing in his stance gave her reason to think the man would interject. "But of course, Lady Sandhurst. You do remember our plans for a wedding trip, do you not?" He leaned forward to snidely whisper into her ear. "Or were you too busy having your lover crawl between your legs to give it much thought?"

Gwendolyn gasped that he would be so crass with her. "He is more of a man than you will ever be, Sandhurst," she replied quietly.

His face turned purple with rage. "You will regret the choices you have made once we are aboard my ship, wife. I promise you shall pay for betraying me."

She smothered a hysterical laugh. "I am not going anywhere with you, and certainly not on any ship."

He smirked. "I was hoping you would say that." He yanked her arm and tossed her at Smith. "Tie the treacherous wench up and gag her . Since she will not go willingly, I have no recourse other than to tie her to her horse and make haste. We have very little time before her brothers come looking for her and realize I have made off with her."

"Sandhurst, do not—" Gwendolyn got no farther. Smith quickly pulled a disgusting rag from who knows where and put it into her mouth. The next thing she knew, rough rope was digging in to her wrists and ankles. Apparently this Smith fellow was wise enough to know she would run at the first opportunity. He picked her up and tossed her over his shoulder to carry her through the forest as though she weighed nothing at all.

He dropped her again when they reached two horses, tied to a tree.

Getting Sandhurst up into the saddle would have been comical if the situation was different. They had wasted precious time when Smith finally was able to hoist him up. As they argued amongst themselves, they decided they needed to hurry. Smith leaned her up against his horse and leap into the saddle before grabbing at the ropes that bound her. She struggled, but could not prevent herself from landing face down across this stranger's lap, her head ready to bounce off the side of the horse at its first movement.

Every clump of sand that flew from the horses' hooves whilst they made their way quickly across the strand took her farther and farther from Berwyck. They must have traveled at least two miles before they reined their horses to a halt. She was tossed over another man's shoulders and shoved into a rowboat. They breasted the choppy waves crashing into the shore, and soon hit calmer water.

Smith, at long last, cut the ropes that had held her. She could hardly climb the ladder of the frigate otherwise. However, her moment of freedom was short-lived. Once her feet hit the deck, she had time for one last look at England's shore, before she was taken below deck to a small cabin and pushed inside. The sound of the door being locked from the outside sealed her fate. She was at her husband's mercy.

TWENTY-TWO

NEVILLE FUMBLED AT his cravat whilst his father's butler poured him a brandy. Taking the glass from the aging man, he nodded his thanks and stared at the amber liquor wishing, not for the first time, that some kind of answer would be found if only he drank himself into oblivion.

He still remembered the moment when Hartford and Worthington had found him on the parapet and informed him Sandhurst had run off with Gwendolyn. Rage had consumed him and it had taken both men to hold him down when he flung himself towards the turret door swearing to bring her back. A cold reminder that Sandhurst was legally her husband and he could take her wherever he so wished, only caused Neville to slam his fist into the wooden door. He had wished it could have been Sandhurst's face.

Gwendolyn had been gone for over a month. In that time, Neville had done his best to continue on with his life, knowing Hartford was doing his part in trying to free her.

He would have been more relieved if he had received some form of word that all was in order. Just to know she was safe, and had returned from wherever she had been taken. The best news, of course, would have been that Gwendolyn was able to marry him, but her safety came first.

"I have never seen you this out of sorts, son, especially over a woman," his father said from across his desk. He never once looked up but continued attending to the business before him.

Neville lifted the glass to his lips and the warmth of the drink went straight to his empty stomach. "She is not your ordinary woman, father."

His father set down the quill with which he had been writing. Lifting his head that had the same auburn hues as Neville's, he leaned forward to rest his elbows on the edge of the desk and clasped his hands to stare sternly at his son. "She is married, Neville."

That voice held the tone of authority that had driven Neville to succeed in everything he ever undertook in his life just to please his father, a father who looked far from happy whilst he gazed upon his son. "I know."

"And…"

Neville sighed. "I still love her and pray her brother, the duke, will soon be able to gain the freedom she so desires from her marriage."

His father reached for his own glass of brandy and swirled the liquid before taking a sip. "The scandal of an annulment or divorce will hit the streets of London and will be hard to live down. Are you sure she is prepared for a scandal that will surely be harder on her than on you?"

"She is a strong woman."

His father set his glass down. "I hope so. She will need

strength, I suspect. The gossipmongers are a vicious lot, much like a pack of wild dogs once they set their teeth into the latest dishonor that falls upon one of *their* own. They will not be kind to her, or you if that matters to you at all. Her birth as the daughter of a duke will only make the rumors spread like wildfire where the two of you are concerned."

"I will take care, father. I can always remove myself to my country house if need be."

"Why do you not take another mistress whilst you wait for her return? At least a woman will keep you occupied and amused until then."

Neville chuckled. "I hardly think taking a mistress will have the benefit you think, father. I have fallen in love. To take another lady to my bed would be to forsake the love of a good woman. Much like what you and mother have together. Surely you would never think of taking a mistress." Neville grinned in amusement.

A snort escaped his sire. "Your mother would see me gelded if she ever found out. Hence, I take no chances. Besides, I am a perfectly happy married man. Why would I need a mistress to see to my pleasures when I am well taken care of?" he laughed.

Neville held up his hands. "Please spare me the details, father, if you do not mind. I hardly want to know how my mother pleases my father when you are abed."

As if she knew she was the subject of their conversation, the study door opened and his mother swept into the room, with Charles following close behind. He stood to greet her, kissing both her cheeks before she started fussing with his untidy cravat.

"I am so glad you are joining us for dinner, Neville." She

graced him with a lovely smile and then laced her arm through his. "It has been far too long since you have come for a visit. What has kept you so occupied that you cannot return home and see your mama?"

Neville began to escort her to the dining room. "I am sincerely sorry for my absence, madam. A matter of grave importance has kept me busy of late." He pulled out her chair and went to take his place at the center seat of the table, and Charles took the chair across from him. Both parents stared at him from opposite ends of the table.

"Ha! How can you be too busy for your own mother? Why, I constantly have to find something to amuse me, since both you and your father are too alike. Business always comes first. I may need to go to my modiste to console myself with a new dress."

"You have enough dresses, my love," his father protested lightly, although Neville knew he would never deny his wife anything she wished.

They began to eat in silence and it was not until they were half way through the second course that his mother set her fork down and picked up her wine. "I think you should go abroad for a while, Neville. A change of scenery will do you good."

"I cannot leave London, mother."

"Of course you can, dear. Your lady will return to you all in good time, I have no doubt of it," she smiled and gave him a wink.

Charles slapped at the table, with a laugh. "A lady? Who is the woman who has finally captured your heart, brother," he questioned.

Neville almost choked on his food. He turned to his father. "You told her?" He would not mention

Gwendolyn's name in case his mother thought unkindly of her, let alone that Charles might put two and two together and realize he had already met the woman.

Before his father could respond, his mother answered for him. "Of a certainty, Neville. Your father does not keep secrets from his wife, especially when they involve one of her sons."

"I repeat, mother, I cannot leave London."

"Then maybe we should have a ball. The season is in full swing. We can entertain to get your mind off your worries." She took another sip of her wine, watching him over the rim of her glass.

"Really, mother, I am not in the mood to be *entertained* by the *ton*."

But it was as though Neville had not spoken a word. His mother began to chatter away about who to invite within Society, rattling off names of those who might come. As if he cared one wit if any of them attended. There was only one woman he wished to see and, until then, he would prefer to be alone to wallow in self-pity. Where the devil had that bastard taken Gwendolyn, and, more importantly, when would she return so he could feel whole again?

TWENTY-THREE

G WENDOLYN BROUGHT A linen handkerchief up to her nose. The slight scent of lavender barely covered the stench of vomit that filled the cabin. At first, she was elated when the ship's motion to and fro caused Sandhurst to heave whatever food he had consumed that day. But as the days turned into weeks, and the weeks into a full month, his health continued to fail from lack of food. Only heaven knew what sustained him; it certainly could not be the small sips of broth she was able to feed him.

She only wished his pride was not so stubborn. His need to pull into port so he could heal was overshadowed by his desire to keep her to himself. He cared not that their marriage was nothing but a farce. At first, he told her they would remain at sea until she could provide proof her monthly courses had arrived and she was not carrying a bastard in her belly. His satisfied laugh when the day arrived caused Gwendolyn to burst into tears. In the back of her mind, she knew it was for the best that she had not conceived, but she would have so loved to have been pregnant with Neville's child.

The door to the cabin had remained unlocked, for where was she to go on board a ship where she was the only female passenger? The times when Sandhurst was coherent enough to allow her above to stretch her legs were brief and rare. She knew going topside was not in her best interest even if her husband owned the vessel, but when Sandhurst permitted it, she still went, needing a breath of fresh air away from this sick room.

The sailors were not pleased to have Sandhurst or her on board. He had only been above a few times when they first started their voyage, but had complained or found fault with whatever he could find. Plus, the crew believed it was bad luck to have a woman on board and that, of course, was her husband's fault as well. She heard them grumbling she was to blame when they encountered a storm. As if she could change the weather.

A knock at the door sounded. "Come in," Gwendolyn called out. She picked up her stitchery. Her workbox had been waiting for her when she arrived, and she was grateful to whoever had packed it. At least she had something to occupy herself during the long days of tending to Sandhurst.

Smith entered along with a cabin boy who replaced the bucket for Sandhurst's use before hastily retreating from the cabin. She could not blame the lad. The stench was unbearable to endure for any length of time.

"Lady Sandhurst," Smith nodded, looking towards the bunk where Sandhurst was sleeping. "Is his lordship any better today?"

"I am afraid not," she answered glaring at the man who had helped with her abduction. "At least he is resting comfortably for now."

"I see," he stood shuffling his feet. "May I have a word with you, my lady, outside?"

Her brow lifted. He thought she would actually wish to have words with him? "Why?"

"Please, your ladyship." Smith sounded contrite and went to open the door for her as if he thought she would agree to speak to him privately. Was the cabin not private enough? Her husband was not in any condition to overhear or care about their conversation.

Curious, she set aside her embroidery. "Very well." At least accompanying this man would get her out of the cabin and into the fresh air.

The ship's passageway was dimly lit and narrow. When she lifted her skirt to manage the stairs, Smith offered his hand to assist her. She refused and once on deck made her way to the railing. *Breathe. Just breathe, Gwendolyn.* She looked out at the wide expanse of open sea. Land was nowhere in sight, the sky overcast and gloomy, much like her mood of late. She had no idea where she was or even in which direction was home. Home. And Neville.

Smith came to stand beside her and she waited for him to speak, as she had no intention of uttering pleasantries in order to make light conversation. He cleared his throat and Gwendolyn turned to face him with a brow raised; a silent command to speak whatever he had on his mind.

Smith shuffled his feet before he gave a heavy sigh. "First, I would like to apologize for the part I played in your being here. I had no idea when I accepted this job what your husband expected of me other than to watch you. I never thought I would aid the man in abducting his own wife, nor be aboard a vessel and gone this long from England. I have a family to take care of back home and thought only of the coin that would see to their needs for many months to come."

"Surely you do not expect me to forgive you?"

"No," he said quietly. "Such forgiveness will be between me and God."

They stood in silence again before Gwendolyn could see there was more on Smith's mind than to say he was sorry. "You might as well tell me whatever you are thinking, Smith. Good or bad, just say it."

Smith nodded. "I have spoken privately with the captain and have told him Lord Sandhurst is incapacitated and unable to make clear decisions due to his illness. Personally, I think the good captain would like nothing better than to return to England and get Sandhurst off the ship."

Gwendolyn's brow rose. "It was presumptuous on your part to speak on behalf of my husband."

"Yes, I know, but I thought perhaps it would somehow make up for the part I played in your being taken away from your family."

"Then why is the captain not heading for home?" Gwendolyn inquired tapping her foot.

"He has his orders to stay out to sea until Sandhurst says otherwise. He did suggest he would be more than willing to pull into any port of your choosing, if you would only instruct him to do so."

Laughter bubbled forth from Gwendolyn. "Me? Why in the world would he take orders from a woman?"

"Since Lord Sandhurst is ill, it is within your rights to see to your husband's health and seek land."

"I still do not see why he would take orders from me when my husband previously refused to pull into port."

"Because when Sandhurst finally leaves this world, then you, my lady, will be the owner of this ship. I believe he would much prefer to stay in your good graces so he is not replaced with another captain because you thought ill of him." Smith sounded confident of his conclusion.

A smile lit Gwendolyn's face. She had never thought far ahead enough to think about what she would gain when Sandhurst was deceased, not daring to consider widowhood would make her free to marry Neville. She did not wish Sandhurst dead despite what he had done to her. His money and property were of no consequence to her, but despite herself, a small flame of hope lit in her heart. Neville had promised to wait a lifetime. Could they be reunited sooner than they thought? No. She would not think it, but she would take Sandhurst and the crew into port.

"I believe, sir, that you may escort me to the captain. I think it is well past time we all returned to our loved ones in England."

Gwendolyn's step was lighter than she could remember since she first boarded this vessel. She was going home.

TWENTY-FOUR

$\mathcal{N}$EVILLE STOOD IN the receiving line of his parent's townhouse welcoming their guests. Once his mother's mind was made up, there was no stopping the woman from proceeding at the speed in which one might expect of a bolt of lightning. It seemed as if invitations had gone out before Neville had even made it back to his own home the day she decided to hold a ball. The last thing he wanted to be doing was standing here being expected to behave as the dutiful son. He did not want to dance the night away with anyone other than the lady of his heart, and yet his mother was demanding such a monumental deed of him.

If he could excuse himself from the growing crowd already in the ballroom, he would have done so. Even as the thought crossed his mind, his father nudged him. Neville could in no way misinterpret the look. Inwardly, he gave a heavy sigh, even whilst he plastered a welcoming smile upon his face and bowed before the next lady who demanded his attention.

Good Lord, not another one who saw nothing but his title and the riches he had amassed for himself. He had seen that look a hundred times before and she would be no different than any of the other grasping women in search of an eligible gentleman to marry. This marriage-bait was a pretty young thing, he would give her that. With her tawny-colored hair and bright blue eyes, she reminded him of summer sunshine. It did not take long, however, for her to ruin his mental image of her, for the little miss of fluff began batting her eyes at him so quickly Neville thought she might actually take flight.

"I do so hope you shall save a dance for me, Lord Drayton," she blatantly cooed, not even waiting for him to do the asking. Not, to be fair, that he would have done so.

What was her name? Ah, yes, Lady Helena Morley, daughter of the viscount who was studying him most earnestly whilst sizing him up as a potential husband for his daughter.

Before he could answer, his mother did so for him. "Of course. Neville would be delighted to take a turn about the dance floor with you, Lady Helena." His mother gave him one of those smiles that told him in no uncertain terms to behave.

He clicked his heels together. "It would be my pleasure."

She gave an annoying giggle that sounded forced to his ears before tapping his arm with her fan. *The brazen chit.* Was this going to be the course of the evening?

Would fathers and mothers parade their marriageable daughters before him all evening long as if he was a ripe prize to be won? He would never survive.

Lady Helena's father came to his rescue, bowing before Neville's mother. "My lady, so kind of you to invite us to your ball. We look forward to the festivities," he declared before escorting his daughter and wife into the ballroom.

A moment's reprieve was welcome, and even more welcome was the sight of none other than the Duke of Hartford, who entered shadowed closely by his brother, with Lady Calliope upon his arm. A hush of silence followed their entrance and those who still remained in the foyer either curtseyed or bowed before His Grace.

Hartford moved past the gawkers attempting to gain the attention of a duke. He waved them off with a ducal stare of indifference and nodded a greeting to Neville's parents. "May we have a private word, Drayton?" He smiled at Neville's mother. "That is, if I may steal you away for a few moments from my hosts for the evening."

Worthington leaned down to whisper in Lady Calliope's ear who nodded her acceptance to whatever he had suggested before entering the ballroom on her own.

Neville did not wait for his parent's consent but began weaving his way through the throng of people who descended upon the foyer like a tidal wave crashing into the shore. The news that a duke of the realm was in attendance had not taken long to reach the ears of the guests who had already been admitted to the ball.

Opening the door to his father's study, Neville allowed Hartford and Worthington to enter but held back the few men who thought to follow the trio. Shutting the door in the men's faces should be proof enough of their need for privacy, and yet Neville took no chance. He locked the door and crossed to the sideboard.

"Have you had word from Gwendolyn?" he inquired, wasting no time by asking how they fared or mouthing trivialities about the current state of the weather. He poured the men a glass of whiskey. "I am under the assumption a drink will be in order since you requested a private word. Was I wrong?"

Worthington reached for his glass and then raised it in a silent toast. "My sister has been back since yesterday."

"Devil take it, Worthington. Why did you not come get me sooner?" Neville downed his drink whilst the brothers did the same. He poured another.

Hartford held out his empty glass as well, and Neville filled it. "Because we knew you would hightail it over to her townhouse with no further thought to the consequences."

"Consequences? To hell with the consequences. I need to assure myself she is unharmed," Neville shouted. His temper that the two brothers would keep their sister isolated from him was exacerbated because he had been consumed with guilt that their time together had caused her harm. He set his glass down, his fists balled at his sides.

Worthington put a hand upon his shoulder. "Calm yourself, Drayton. She is fine. A little shaken, but otherwise she will be her normal self in no time."

"Under the circumstances, I advise you to let her come to you when the time is right." Hartford's firm tone suggested this was more of an order than anything else.

Neville rubbed his eyes. "What are you not telling me, gentlemen?"

The two brothers looked at one another before Worthington spoke up. "Sandhurst is ill. The doctor says he will not live much longer. The sea voyage apparently took its toll on the man."

"I may not care for Sandhurst, but I would not wish any ill on another soul," Hartford added, tossing back his drink. "Even one who abducted my sister against her will. But how will it look if you go traipsing over to her house whilst Sandhurst is on his death bed? You must think of her reputation, and your own, of course."

"Confound it, Hartford! You cannot expect me to just sit here and not do everything in my power to see the woman I love," Neville swore.

Hartford smirked. "Of course I do not expect you to just sit here. I expect you to leave this room and enjoy the ball your parents are giving. Dance, flirt with any of the available young ladies, play a game of cards with the other gentlemen, smoke a cigar. I do not care what you do, as long as you wait to see my sister until the time is appropriate."

Neville was sure the blood in his veins was about to boil over at the injustice of it all. "Damnation!"

Worthington set his empty glass down before pulling out a sealed envelope and handing it to him. "We are not completely heartless, Drayton, although you may think so at the moment. She asked that we personally deliver this to you."

Neville's hand trembled when he took the parchment from Worthington.

"We shall leave you to it, then," Hartford said, heading towards the door. "Join me for cards, Drayton, when you are ready. I have the feeling Brandon will be escorting a certain young lady about the dance floor for a turn or two."

The two brothers left and Neville sank into a nearby chair. She was home. The faintest hint of lavender came from the envelope he held. He raised the parchment to his nose and inhaled, assailed by memories of Gwendolyn in the throes of passion whilst she lay naked in his bed. He took a deep breath and broke the wax seal to read her words.

> *My Dearest Neville,*
>
> *Not a single day has passed when I have not thought of you. I pray this letter finds you well and you will not think too harshly of me when I ask you to give my situation the time that is needed. I think only of our families when I make such a request, so as not to bring shame upon us. Be at ease and know I have not been harmed and am anxious to be held again in your arms. I beg of you, please be patient until we are reunited again and never forget how much I love you.*
>
> *Most fondly,*
> *Gwendolyn*

Neville sighed, tucking her letter into his jacket. Her note was not overly long but her words were enough. Patience. She had asked him to be patient. It had never been one of his stronger virtues. He would do the best he could and listen to her brother's advice.

He downed the remainder of his drink and headed for the door to play his part for the amusement of others. In the card room, he rather thought. Maybe if he fleeced Hartford out of some of his coins, he might feel a bit more cheerful. It was better than dancing attendance on some flippant miss with wedding bells shining in her eyes.

TWENTY-FIVE

*G*WENDOLYN SET THE book down in her lap at the sound of a soft knock at the door. Sandhurst still slept and she quietly made her way across her husband's room. Opening the door, she saw the kitchen maid holding a tray. She motioned the girl to set the tray down near the hearth.

"Hollis thought you might like something to eat, milady," the maid stated and set to work stoking the fire. "There is also some broth for his lordship when he awakens."

"Thank you, Agatha," Gwendolyn murmured, then proceeded to pour herself a cup of tea. She stared at the array of food before her and was unsure how she would get anything besides the hot brew past her lips. "Please convey my gratitude to Hollis as well."

"Of course, milady. Can I be of any further service?"

She patted Agatha's shoulder but began ushering her towards the door. "There is nothing more you can do for me at this time. I will ring if I have need of anything."

With the closing of the door, she heard Sandhurst moving upon the bed. His cold eyes seared into her as though he were once again wishing her to the devil. She made her way back to the hearth and took hold of the bowl of broth, bringing it to the bedside. Sandhurst attempted to sit up with difficulty. The little bit of effort caused him to double over in a wracking fit of coughs. She set the bowl down and began adjusting the pillows behind him, but he swatted her hand away to reject her attempt at providing him with comfort.

Gwendolyn sat back down in her chair near his bed, waiting for him to finally settle himself into a comfortable position. Bringing her chair closer, she took up the bowl and offered him a spoonful of broth. Sandhurst managed to swallow more than he dribbled down his chin and she offered him another sip. Taking up a napkin, she dabbed at his mouth to clean him as best as possible. He was burning with fever.

"Enough!" Bernard hissed in a raspy voice. "I have had enough of your coddling."

"We should call the doctor again, my lord," Gwendolyn declared. Sitting back in her chair, she attempted to assess how she could help him if he would not listen to her advice.

"Bah! That old sawbones Doctor Thornberry your family sent for cannot do anything more for me and you very well know it."

"That is because you refuse to listen to his counsel. In order for you to be well, you should be heeding the good doctor's orders. He has been at the call of our family for as long as I can remember. I value his judgment and wish you would heed his suggestions for your care."

Anger blazed in his eyes once more. "You do not give a

damn for my care, wife, so let us cut this attempt at pleasantries between us."

"You are still my husband. You may not believe me, but I do not bear ill will towards you or wish you any harm, my lord."

"By God! I am at death's door and still you refuse to use my name," he bellowed, which brought on a spate of coughing that took his breath away.

Gwendolyn swallowed hard, affected by the misery she heard in his voice. She took a deep breath. The man appeared as though he had one foot inside death's door. She could do this, if it would ease his suffering. "Bernard, I—"

Laughter was not what she expected. "You think to console your soul by trying now to be a complacent wife? It is a little too late for that, do you not think, my pet?"

"I am a Christian woman, my lord," she answered with a lift of her chin. She would try to be compassionate towards the sick man before her, but if her last words with this man were to be an argument, then so be it..

"Ha! You are a traitorous wife and an adulteress. Let us not play games on my deathbed, Gwen," he sneered.

"For that I shall seek forgiveness with prayer and before the eyes of God, but I am not sorry for trying to find the smallest measurement of happiness for myself."

A snort escaped him. "How contradictory. You seek God's forgiveness for something that is a sin in His eyes, and yet you are not truly sorry in the least for your actions."

"A person cannot help where their heart leads them, Bernard, or with whom they fall in love."

"Love… such an emotion does not exist. Your own dearly departed father knew you would never love me, but I forced his hand by calling in his debt."

"What?" Gwendolyn searched her husband's face and saw a fair amount of satisfaction etched there.

"How else do you think I could wed a duke's daughter? You were so young you were not even aware your father was on the brink of financial ruin. You did not even come with a dowry, but I did not care. I thought in time you could come to have a small amount of affection for me, fool that I was. I took care of your father's immediate debts and basically paid him for the right to wed you in return for keeping him and you all from being forced to beg in the streets. Blackmail always gets you what you most want in life. Why do you think Hartford works so tirelessly trying to redeem your family's financial wealth and good name? It is because I threatened him with revealing to the *ton* the true nature of your father's ruin."

"I had no idea the situation had been so dire," Gwendolyn whispered. It all made sense now and poor Edmond. At such a young age to be hiding they were practically paupers, along with the burden of restoring what once had been a thriving duchy.

"Hartford tried to dissuade me from carrying out my threats to expose the true nature of the deal your father and I had made," Bernard added, "but I wanted you no matter the cost. Too bad it was all for naught."

"How so?" she inquired watching the man as if seeing him for the first time.

Sadness enveloped him as though he had given up on life and Gwendolyn watched the color drain from his face. Bernard slid down further into his bed to stare up at the ceiling. "I leave nothing behind. No heir to continue my name and a wife I could never physically love. Life has been but a cruel joke where I am concerned."

"Life is a gift, Bernard, if you only choose to enjoy what it has to offer," she murmured reaching out to take his hand.

He turned to face her with a sly smile and gave an eerie laugh. "My life has been a living hell. But I will have my revenge," he declared. This time, when he began coughing, droplets of blood were left at the corners of his mouth. He yanked at her hand in a surprisingly strong grip. "Just remember, Gwendolyn dear, I will always be watching you, even after I take my last breath. Perhaps if I haunt you in the afterlife, I will then have the last laugh. You and your damn lover can rot in hell…" Bernard's voice trailed off after his eerie declaration.

Before Gwendolyn could even utter a reply, her husband expelled his last slow breath. He continued to stare at her with sightless eyes until she took her hand from his and shut them. Sitting back in her chair again, she watched as deathly pallor consumed her husband and his skin quickly turned a pasty grey.

With a sigh of resignation, she rose and went to summon Hollis to ready the house for a state of mourning and to call for a clergyman. She could have sworn, after one last backward glance towards the man lying dead in his bed, she could hear his cackle of laughter inside her head.

TWENTY-SIX

*G*WENDOLYN WAS NUMB and past caring about anything other than making it through another day. Relief was overshadowed with guilt that she had somehow been the cause of her husband's demise. She knew such thoughts were foolish and yet they continued to besiege her mind every day since she had once again put her feet on English soil.

She barely heard the priest uttering prayers of reverence over Sandhurst's remains. Even whilst staring at his coffin ready to be placed in the ground, she could not think of him by his first name, despite giving in to calling him 'Bernard' on his deathbed.

What sort of woman could not say her husband's name? Perhaps she was attempting to ease her guilty conscience by going to her husband's burial site. This was not a normal custom for a woman of her station, but she had insisted even though Brandon and Edmond had urged her to stay home.

Her gaze swept the dozen or so people who had shown up for his funeral. Their attendance did not say much for a man who had lived a long life, for they were few, and Gwendolyn knew hardly anyone; none who she would call a friend. At least Sandhurst had people here to pay their last respects. She supposed some were better than none at all.

She brought a handkerchief up under the heavy black veil that cast her face into shadows. This public display would show she was despondent over the death of her spouse. If she must feign she had an ounce of pity or actually cared about him, then so be it. She supposed this would be just another thing to add to the list of her transgressions when she prayed to God for the forgiveness of her sins.

She wiped at her eyes. They were as dry as her emotions. She attempted to conjure up at least a sniffle or two for appearances sake, but it was no use. Appearances. It was always about how you appeared to the outside world looking in. When it came to Society, just one slip in your composure and the next thing you knew, your name was splattered across the gossip column in the *Morning Post*.

She glanced up at the sound of those around her speaking a soft amen. She mumbled the word herself, whilst shame overwhelmed her that she had not paid the least bit of attention to the prayers. Sandhurst was in God's hands now and may his soul rest in peace. Gwendolyn knew it was a sin not to forgive the man for his trespasses against her. She supposed she would pay the price for that and all her other transgressions when her own time came to meet her maker.

"Lady Sandhurst." The clergyman said her name to gain her attention when she once again became lost in her own musings.

"Here, Gwendolyn," her brother Brandon whispered, handing her a blood red rose. She stared at the flower as though it was offensive whilst the scent from the bloom almost made her gag.

Putting one foot in front of the other, Gwendolyn stood looking down upon the coffin before carefully placing the rose on it. Edmond came to stand next to her and repeated the gesture then took her elbow for support. They began to slowly make their way to the waiting carriage. Brandon would stay for the rest of the interment, but Edmond would escort her home. At least her brother knew she had had enough and could no longer stand there whilst the others paid their last respects.

A footman came to open the door for her and she had just placed her foot on the step when she was overcome by a feeling of being watched. Refusing her brother's hand, she swept her gaze across the surrounding area and swiveled back to stare at the lone man leaning one shoulder up against a tree some distance from where she stood. She would have recognized Neville anywhere. Her breath hitched to be so close to him and yet so far away. He reached up and tipped his hat then placed has hands behind his back. He might as well have been a statue made of marble, for he stood so very still. Alone. Watching no one but her.

Subconsciously, she took a step forward to join him but a hand held her back. Her brow rose at her brother's audacity.

"Get in the carriage, Gwendolyn." Edmond's voice was firm with resolve.

"But—"

"Now is not the time, Gwendolyn. Get in the carriage," he repeated crisply.

With a heavy sigh, she stepped into the carriage only to peer out the window, knuckles white from holding stiffly onto its edge. Pulling back her veil, she gave Neville the briefest of nods. Her heart leapt when he took his hand to place it over his heart. She could have stared at him for the rest of her life, yet, with the blink of her eyes, he was gone.

She glared at her brother, furious. "How could you not let me speak with him, Edmond?" she fumed, not trusting herself to say more for fear it would damage the fragile truce between them.

"And have the gossipmongers bandying about how Sandhurst barely had one foot in the grave and already his widow was sizing up her next husband?" Edmond muttered through clenched teeth.

"As if they care what I do or as if I care what they think," Gwendolyn murmured gazing out the window again as the few people at the gravesite began to disperse.

"*I* care what you do, Gwen. If you have no care for your own reputation, then at least think of the family's."

Her brow rose at his implication that she cared not for her family. "Of course, let us not forget how important our reputation is to Society." She scowled. "I was just starting to like you again, Hartford. Will I need to go into seclusion for the full year of mourning or will you at least allow me to see the light of day from time to time?"

"You try my patience, Gwen. Leave it be, at least for a day," he warned. "I am not in the mood for you to chastise me for a slight that could not be avoided."

"Marrying me off to a man who was twice my age just because father made such an arrangement condemned me to months of verbal, emotional, and physical abuse, Hartford."

Edmond sighed, suddenly looking tired and older than his years. "You gave your consent, if you recall."

"As if you need to remind me. I cannot even begin to tell you the more intimate details of such a relationship other than to say my life was a living hell," she retorted through tight lips. She gave a heavy sigh. Shame once more flooded her as she wondered just how far in debt the family really had been that Edmond had no choice than to honor the commitment to her marriage.

"I am sorry, Edmond, to sound like an ungrateful shrew. It breaks my heart to only guess the struggles you must have gone through to save our family from financial ruin."

"Sandhurst told you." There was an underlying tone to Edmond's words and Gwendolyn reached out for her brother's hand.

"Yes and I am sorry for my part in adding to your troubles."

Edmond mumbled his own apology for his part in her horrific marriage but said no more on the matter. Gwendolyn leaned back into her seat to gaze out the window. Neville caught her eye again as he made his way to his carriage. He gave one last look in her direction, nodded, and then disappeared inside his conveyance. His coachman shut the door. Before she could even take another breath, he was gone yet again.

"You will see him again soon, Gwen. I have no doubt of it," Edmond declared, as though he knew where her thoughts had gone.

"A year is a long time to wait for someone," she grumbled, leaning her head back into her seat and closing her eyes. She was trying her best not to panic.

Edmond reached over and took her hand. "I am certain Drayton believes you will be worth the wait."

Gwendolyn began to doubt everything. Her life was once again spiraling out of control around her, confounding her brief sense she had any power to twist it to her whim. No. She must not think like that. She would just need to exercise a fair amount of patience, much as she told Neville to do. She must wait; wait and pray the love she had found with the man who had stolen her heart would not be lost over time.

TWENTY-SEVEN

*T*IME HAD BECOME his enemy. He had too much of it on his hands. He made every attempt to return to his normal lifestyle before he had met the beautiful Gwendolyn. *Normal... Bah! What was normal about his life of late*, he pondered? His heart was certainly not into the usual gentlemanly pursuits he used to enjoy so much. Gambling, riding, or visiting his clubs held no appeal. Everything that used to give him pleasure had become meaningless attempts to make time pass more quickly. The thought of taking another mistress never crossed his mind.

Neville took a sip of his drink whilst he continued staring into the flames within his hearth. He had moved to his country estate right after Sandhurst's funeral, determined he would not stay in London if he could not be near the woman he loved. His mother had fretted to no end that he was closing his townhouse when the Season had only just begun. His servants had merely packed up and honored his whim to leave London behind.

Had that been a mistake? Most likely. At least if he had remained in town, he might espy the fair lady from time to time. But what good did that do him? Gwendolyn would be in seclusion for some time yet. Winter had already come and gone but she would still be in mourning for several more months. He was not sure he could stand waiting much longer, although there really was no choice, if he wished to one day marry the woman without the *ton* ripping their reputations to shreds. He did not wish to bring shame upon their families, but remembering his lady's written words to be patient was no easy task.

The rapid staccato of heels crossing the marble foyer echoed eerily, disrupting his melancholy mood. He only prayed his mother had not sought him out to convince him to return to town. He had no plans to oblige her today, nor any date in the future. His disposition sunk even lower at the thought of putting on a face to show Society all was well in his corner of the world.

"No need to announce me. I can find him myself, thank you."

Neville rose. That silky familiar voice was the last sound he expected to hear in the countryside; nor had he thought she would have the nerve to intrude upon his solitude here of all places. "What the devil are you doing here, Cassandra?" he inquired with furrowed brow when his ex-mistress swept into the room. His question hung in the air between them and he watched her face fall whilst her eyes narrowed in irritation that he did not make her feel welcome.

"You cad, Drayton. Is that anyway to greet me?" she purred sweetly, setting a mask of disinterest across her features that dispelled any thoughts she was truly cross with him. She sashayed across the remaining space between them and stood upon the tips of her toes to press a soft kiss upon his cheek.

"Considering we ended our association months ago, I believe my question is more than reasonable," he grumbled. He continued to stare at her, trying to figure out her reason for intruding upon his desire for privacy.

"I am here to see you. Is that not obvious, darling?" Cassandra proceeded to throw her pelisse onto a nearby chair. Her reticule carelessly joined the garment. The lady then went to sit in a chair before the fire. Her fan slipped open in an artful display. Cassandra was a woman who knew how to use such an accessory to her advantage whilst she perused him. She began waving her latest acquisition before her face, fluttering her eyelashes at him as if to say she would once more welcome him into her bed. "Pour me something to fortify me after that dreadful trip in a coach to reach you."

"I hope you had the driver wait, my dear. I have no intention of picking up where we left off." His voiced dripped his disdain that she was present in his home.

"Ha! I am not here for that," she stated, snapping her fan shut with enough force to break it in two. "Really, Drayton. Are you not even the slightest bit happy to see me?"

He made his way to the sideboard and poured a draught of sherry into a glass. Returning, he handed it to her. Taking a seat opposite her, he reached for his own glass and took a sip. "What do you want, Cassandra?" he asked, not bothering to answer her question.

"I can see you are in no mood for pleasantries, so I will get to the point of my visit."

A snort escaped him. "How refreshing."

She peered at him over the rim of her drink. "I was told

you were out of sorts and I must admit I had a laugh that people might think you were not your normal self. I could not believe what I had heard when I was told you, of all people, would be languishing away in seclusion because of the loss of some woman. But I can see what I thought an outlandish tale was not a falsehood."

"And just who would be telling you something so personal in nature, my dear?" he inquired with raised brow. At least she had the decency to blush. He swore it was the first time he had ever witnessed her do so.

"A mutual acquaintance." Her answer was quietly muffled as she took another sip of her sherry.

His brow rose yet again. There were only two men who knew of his association with Gwendolyn. "You are bedding Hartford, I take it? Not that it matters."

Cassandra took another sip before setting her glass down. A grimace marred her otherwise beautiful face. "No, the arrogant cur. Why the man lifted his aristocratic nose at me as if I was beneath him when I suggested a liaison."

Neville chuckled, not voicing the obvious that the man was a duke and the lady before him was, for a fact, far beneath him, as far as Society was concerned. "I see. You have gone for the younger brother then," he surmised, although he briefly wondered what had happened with Worthington and the very available Lady Calliope.

"He is refreshingly pleasant and will do nicely for however long he decides to stay around. But whom I take to my bed is not the reason I am here."

"Then by all means, please enlighten me so you may be on your way," he scowled. "I have only so much patience these days and care not to be reprimanded by you or anyone else for not remaining in London."

Cassandra looked around his hall with a critical eye as though she had not heard him. "I cannot believe you are sulking here in the countryside, Drayton. Good Lord, you are sitting in a musty old castle with a moat, for heaven's sake, and during the height of the Season. Whatever could you be thinking?"

"There are not enough words to express how happy I am that you so whole heartedly approve of my estate, Cassandra," he scoffed. "I do not see how it is yours or anyone's business what I do with my personal life."

"Do you love her?"

Her question startled him. "What?"

"You heard me. Worthington's sister… do you love her?" she repeated. Her smile hinted that she was pleased to know who had finally stolen his heart.

"What does it matter if I love her or not?" he complained bitterly. "It is not as if I can run off to London to claim her whilst she is in mourning."

"Why not?" A simple question and yet Neville was unclear why she even bothered to ask when the answer was so obvious.

"Society would never allow us to show our heads again, that is why."

"What rubbish you spout, Drayton. When did you ever give a fig about what the *ton* thought of you or your reputation for that matter?" She took a sip of her drink and continued peering at him over the rim of the crystal. Her eyes sparkled with delight to see him so obviously uncomfortable.

"You know how vicious Society can be, especially when they get their hooks into the latest gossip for them to chew on over their morning tea. I will not subject Gwendolyn to their ridicule."

"I see..." her voice trailed away but they lingered in the heated air between them. "So it has finally happened."

"What has happened? Am I missing some part of this conversation?" he asked. He didn't know what Cassandra meant; nor could he discern her motive.

Her laughter rang out causing him to shudder. "Why, Neville, darling. Do you not even know when you have fallen in love, my dearest?"

"I am not *your* dearest." He rose, reaching out a hand to steady the chair that almost fell over in his haste to put whatever distance he could between himself and the irksome woman who should not be present in his home in the first place. "You have a habit, Cassandra, of irritating me. Sometimes I believe you do it just to see how far you can push me."

"Yet, here I still am, comfortably seated in your hall and not cast out on my way back to London." She laughed again but the sound died when she saw he would not share her mirth. She finished her sherry and retrieved her pelisse. She handed the garment over to him and presented her back, allowing him to place the cloak upon her shoulders. She turned to face him and waited.

"I will think on your words," he said gruffly.

Her hand reached up to touch his cheek. He remained motionless. "She is a lucky woman," Cassandra sighed as her hand fell to her side. "Do yourself a favor, Neville. Get yourself to London and go fetch your lady, so you can be happy. You deserve to be happy."

"But Society—"

"Can go hang," she finished smartly. "I hope you are smart enough to realize the only thing that really matters is the two of you being together. I am certain once you do, then everything warring inside your head about what you think is *proper* will not matter whatsoever."

"We shall see," he murmured. "I wish you the best, Cassandra. I do not have to tell you not to return here, do I?"

As she gazed upon him, Neville saw a moment's hesitation. "No, Drayton. You need not worry about me returning. Be well and happy, sir."

"And the same to you," he stated, with the briefest of nods.

As Cassandra left, Neville once more fell into his chair. He took up his glass and continued staring at what was left of the contents. Yet his fears for Gwendolyn's reputation still kept him from acting on his instincts for another fortnight before he realized he needed to settle his affairs. Nothing would resolve itself while he moped around his countryside estate. With his decision made, Neville ordered his clothes packed and the coach to be brought around. It was time to put his life back in order.

TWENTY-EIGHT

$\mathcal{G}$ WENDOLYN LIFTED THE black veil from the mirror and stared upon her reflection. Her face was gaunt. Her eyes were dull and lifeless. It was as though the dark gowns of mourning and the mood of the house had transformed her into a shadow of her former self. She let the material fall back into place, afraid one of the servants might see that she had been disrespectful for lifting the drapery in the first place.

Perhaps Edmond was right. He kept telling her she should move out of this depressing house. The memories found in the darkened corners of the manor only deepened her melancholy mood. Every room seemed to carry the haunting presence of Sandhurst, lingering in the air as though he was indeed watching her every move. His words, muttered on his last dying breath, whisked across her soul like a grim reminder he would haunt even her waking hours. She shivered. His vow upon his deathbed was almost a premonition. Ever since, she had been constantly looking over her shoulder for his shadow to scare her to pieces. She swore she would not allow his ghost the satisfaction of seeing her fall apart, especially for the rest of her life.

"Do come and sit down, Gwen, and have a cup of tea," Calliope declared. She placed a splash of milk in a cup before holding up the offering for Gwendolyn to take.

With a heavy sigh, Gwendolyn paced the room. "I am not in the mood for tea, Callie."

"Well, it is a little early in the day to be drinking something stronger, but I am sure we can accommodate you. Shall I ring for one of the servants to bring you some wine or sherry if that is your preference?"

Gwendolyn went to the window and pulled back the curtain. Spring was in the air and she would like nothing more than to shed her mourning garb and run out to enjoy the sunny weather. "No. I am in need of nothing," she answered, before closing the drapery again. She took another look around the dismal room and clutched the back of a chair whilst her dear friend continued to stare at her.

Calliope finally put the teacup back on the trolley. "When was the last time you ate something?" she demanded.

"I do not remember."

"Honestly, Gwen, you cannot continue to go on like this. Where has my friend gone? You always had more gumption than most women I know?"

"I believe my marriage may have stolen such an attribute from me," Gwendolyn replied. She began her pacing again. Of late, she had felt as though she was a caged animal, which was not far from the truth.

"For heaven's sake, sit down. You are making me nauseous with this constant going back and forth."

Gwendolyn finally complied and took a seat next to Calliope. Lifting her teacup, she took a sip and had to admit the brew tasted wonderful. "I do not know why you put up with me," she murmured softly.

Calliope reached over to grasp Gwendolyn's hand. "I *put up with you* because you and I have known each other for as long as I can remember. There has never been a time in our lives where we did not come to call when there was a need. Well... with the exception of when your husband banished me from your house and refused to allow me to speak with you." She took a look around this room and shuddered. "If there was ever a moment you could use a friend, such a time is certainly now."

"You read my mind, Callie, and I am so sorry about that nasty business with Sandhurst," Gwendolyn replied. "I was in such a rotten mood, I did not want to bother you with the sorry state my life had become."

"You need to get out of this house, dearest. I do not wish to speak ill of the dead, but this place holds too many memories better left in the past. You cannot, in good conscience, start a new life if your old one is hanging over your head."

Gwendolyn choked back a sob. "Start a new life? How can I when I will be in mourning for months to come? Society will—"

"To *hell* with Society," Calliope bellowed. Her voice echoed off the walls of the salon, and her eyes darted to the entryway as if in embarrassment at how the sound had travelled. Then she leaned forward to say, quietly, "What about Lord Drayton?"

"Shhh!" Gwendolyn whispered, frantic his name would somehow makes its way to the gossipmongers.

"No one is around to hear our conversation," Calliope muttered, taking up her tea again. "You deserve to be happy. Life is fragile, like snowflakes clustered upon the leaves of a tree. With the warmth of the sun, they melt into water to be taken away on the slightest hint of a breeze. You have to grab after the opportunities life presents you, with all haste before they disappear."

"Being philosophical is not going to make me feel any better," Gwendolyn snapped watching as her friend's brow rose.

"No? I should think you would heed my words and grasp whatever bit of happiness you can find. I am most certain you could have a wonderful life with your earl."

"I cannot contact Neville Quinn."

"I do not see why not, but that is the choice you shall have to live with. If you refuse to send him a note, then for heaven's sake, get out of this house. You are more than welcome to stay with me or I am sure your mother would not mind a trip to Berwyck. You always did love that castle, despite the fact it is so far north."

For an instant, pleasant memories of her time at Berwyck with Neville took precedence over the horrible ones where her own husband had taken her hostage. "You may have a point," Gwendolyn conceded. She watched her friend give her an I-told-you-so look. "You do not have to be so smug about it."

"Getting away from here should have been a relatively easy conclusion given the way these walls tend to close in, even on me. You should sell the place, or hand it over to one of your brothers so they can deal with it." Calliope stood and began putting on her gloves.

"You are leaving?" Gwendolyn asked quietly.

"I have dinner plans along with the theater tonight."

"I must really be behind in what is going on with your life. I was not aware you were seeing anyone. Is it serious?"

Calliope gave her a sheepish look. "I cannot say the relationship, if that is what it can even be called, is serious, Gwen. It is just dinner and the theater. Besides, Brandon does not seem at all inclined to settle down anytime soon, so I am not getting my hopes up that anything will come of it. All the same, I am not getting any younger, and if I cannot find a husband of my own soon, my parents will take the choice from me."

"My brother?" Gwen choked out with a laugh.

"I hope you do not object."

"Of course not, Callie, I simply do not want to see you get hurt," Gwen replied. She knew what a carefree rake Brandon could be. "Why do you not, perhaps, accompany me up north."

Calliope enveloped her in a hug. "You do not need me as your companion, dear. You already know what you need to do. Leave this place, along with its repulsive memories, and start your life anew. I shall be here once you can think clearly and return to town again."

Gwendolyn kissed her cheek and, leaving the fragrance of her perfume lingering in the air, Callie was gone. Gwendolyn went back to her tea, but the brew had already turned cold, much like her thoughts now that she was once more alone.

A door slammed and Gwendolyn jumped out of her chair as the sound drove visions of her dead husband into her already tortured mind. Yes. She had to leave this house. Her decision made, she pulled on the bell cord to summon Hollis who appeared as if he were only awaiting her to need his services.

"You rang, madam?" he asked keeping his face masked of any emotion.

Gwendolyn went to the writing desk set up by the window and hastily picked up a quill to write her message. "Yes, Hollis. Efficient as ever I see?"

"I do try, my lady."

Finishing her note, she took up the red wax, heated it over a candle and then proceeded to seal it with her stamp. "Please ensure this is delivered promptly to my mother. I will be heading to Berwyck. Please also ready the carriage for a long trip north."

"As you wish, madam."

"And please have my maid start packing my things. Ginny will know what I stand in need of. I wish to depart within the hour."

He hesitated only briefly, no doubt to assess her urgency to leave the household and the memories it contained.

"I will summon her myself to see the job completed as you desire, Lady Sandhurst," he replied heading toward the door.

"Hollis…" she called, and watched him turn once more in her direction. "You have been good to me, and I appreciate the kindness you have shown considering the circumstances in which I was placed. Although I am uncertain what I plan to do with the house, I will be sure you are not put out without the best recommendation I can provide you and the rest of the staff."

"It has been my pleasure to be of service to your ladyship."

Hollis left without another word, leaving Gwendolyn to her own thoughts. With one last look about the room, she rushed up the stairs in order to leave this house once and for all. As far as she was concerned, her departure from this place could not happen soon enough.

TWENTY-NINE

EVILLE PULLED BACK on the reins of his
borrowed horse, halting the steed on a small rise,
the small village of Berwyck behind him. The view was
remarkable and he was certain *this* was the reason
Gwendolyn had returned home. Home… Neville could not
imagine living in any dwelling, be it a castle or a hovel,
without Gwendolyn there to make the place worthy of
being called by that most dear and familiar name.

Berwyck Castle rose majestically from a cliff overlooking
the vast ocean. Neville could well imagine knights of old
standing tall and proud upon the battlement walls. A banner
with a fire-breathing dragon flew high from the roof of the
keep, signifying the duchy. With a flick of the reins, Neville
set his horse back into motion, eager to be near the woman
he loved. The field between the village and the castle seemed
endless, yet he made quick work of lessening the distance to
the barbican gate.

The clip clop of the horse's hooves as he made his way

over the drawbridge echoed in the air whilst the sun chose that moment to shine directly into Neville eyes. As he went to shield the sun from his vision, he thought he caught a glimpse of a knight standing at the entryway to the castle; one who gave Neville a jaunty salute with his blade. He blinked and the vision was gone, but Neville swore he heard the sound of a sword being returned to a scabbard as he went beneath the portcullis. He shook his head to clear such fanciful thoughts. Obviously, his imagination was getting the better of him.

As he entered the bailey, a stable lad came to take his horse and Neville made his way up the stairs to the keep wondering how he would be received. Would Gwendolyn come rushing down the Great Hall's turret stairs in her eagerness to see him, or would he be turned out by some servant at her request? He knew she was still in mourning but he would delay no longer to claim his lady. He had waited long enough.

He had barely raised his hand to use the knocker when a livered footman opened the door wide, a promising sign if he ever saw one.

"Her Grace will see you, my lord, in the Great Hall," the man stated. He motioned with his arm to enter.

Neville stood rooted to the spot, unable to take a step into the keep. He had not expected to see Gwendolyn's mother, at least at this particular place and time.

"This way, sir," the servant urged, causing Neville to come out of his stupor of indecision. He supposed such a meeting was inevitable if he were to become part of their family in the not too distant future. His feet felt heavy as he followed behind the footman, who began escorting him through the room toward the massive fireplace. With the briefest of introductions, the servant left him with Gwendolyn's mother. The only sound in the room was the snapping and crackling of the logs burning in the hearth.

"Good afternoon, Your Grace," Neville stated as he bowed. He could see where Gwendolyn received her looks. Her mother was still a beautiful woman with only a hint of grey in her otherwise dark black hair. Eyes the color of steel grey openly judged him.

"Lord Drayton, do be seated." The duchess had been in the process of pouring a cup of tea from a trolley near at hand. She held the cup out to him, which he took after he sat in the chair opposite her. "I have been expecting you."

Her words surprised him. "You have?"

A small smile cracked her face and her brow rose. "Yes, of course. I can only wonder why it took you so long to come to the conclusion you should seek out my daughter." She took a sip of her tea, waiting for his answer.

Neville set his teacup down. "She is in mourning. I thought, given the circumstances, it would be wise for me to refrain from allowing the gossipers of London to drag Gwendolyn's name through the mud by seeking her out sooner."

"Her marriage to Lord Sandhurst was not what most would consider a happy one," she stated, watching him closely.

"I am aware of the situation, Your Grace. To be honest I am surprised you would sanction my being here at all, let alone you would allow me to converse with your daughter before her mourning period is over."

The Duchess of Hartford set her tea down and began drumming her fingers on one of the arms of her chair. "Did I say I was allowing you to speak to my daughter, my lord?

I must have missed that part of our brief conversation."

Did it, of a sudden, grow excessively warm in this infernal room? Neville swore his cheeks reddened in embarrassment at his assumption. "My apologies, my lady. I should never have assumed you would allow me to take such a liberty with your daughter."

"Hmmm... and yet, I have the distinct feeling you may have already done as much or more, Lord Drayton, most likely in this very castle."

Neville's cravat seemed as though it tightened around his neck under the close scrutiny of this very observant lioness of a mother defending one of her cubs. His mouth opened to justify his actions, but the lady before him silenced him by holding up one delicate hand. He snapped his lips shut before he made a bigger fool of himself. He knew this had been a mistake. He only waited for the lady before him to summon some burly footman to oust him from Berwyck.

"Lord Drayton... May I be frank?"

"Of course, your ladyship."

The duchess leaned forward in her chair. "Do you love my daughter?"

"That I am here should be enough of an answer, but, yes, I love her very much." Neville continued to hold Gwendolyn's mother's stare so this woman would have no doubt her daughter's happiness was his main concern.

Was she satisfied with his answer? He was uncertain whilst she continued to look him up and down assessing his worth. The duchess at last sat back and took up her tea again. "I shall, of course, act as a chaperone for my daughter while you are here. She has had a difficult time dealing with the sudden death of her husband, and yet I understand the dilemma you both face. I am certain she loves you as much as you claim you love her."

Neville gave the woman before her a simple nod. "You give me hope for our future, my lady."

"Where there is love, there is always hope, Neville. You do not mind if I call you by your given name considering you hope to become a part of this family."

"I am honored, Your Grace."

A distant cry of alarm echoed eerily from the turret stairs causing Neville to jump to his feet. He looked askance to the duchess.

"She has been having nightmares of late. She will not speak of them to me but perhaps she will confide in you about what haunts her dreams. You may seek her out for yourself; with my permission, of course. I am certain you know the way."

"You have no objection to my being alone with her?" Neville asked in amazement at such a lack of convention.

"She is not alone. If she was, I would accompany you to her room. I sent for Lady Calliope who has been attending her." Her Grace gave a wave of her hand, motioning towards the stairwell.

One moment, Neville was bowing low to Gwendolyn's mother, and the next he was taking the stairs two at a time. He did, indeed, know the way to his lady's room and—hopefully—her heart.

THIRTY

F IRE INCHED ITS *way closer and closer to where she stood. Bernard laughed as his clothes became consumed in the very same flames that would surely drag her down into the depths of hell. He reached for her but she stepped back, only to run into a wall of stone that for some unknown reason felt only warm to the touch. She would have thought that the devil's den would be scorching hot, especially since the demon had apparently claimed her soul.*

"I told you I would haunt you forever, my dear," Bernard cackled. "You and your lover shall never be together. Face it, wife, you shall be tied to me for all of eternity."

"No," she screamed out, but the sound of her voice sounded weak, even to her own ears. "Neville will save me and you shall never touch me ever again."

Her husband laughed again and seemingly grew in size. "How wrong you are, my dear traitorous wife. You belong to me and only me. Welcome to hell…"

Gwendolyn sobbed, and, in her tormented mind, she called out over and over to the one person who she knew would breach hell to reach her side…

"Neville!"

Gwendolyn lurched up in her bed, even as her bedroom door burst open with a crash. Callie was holding her hand offering her comfort. With tears streaming down her wet cheeks, she knew she yet dreamed. How else could Neville be here, at Berwyck, of all places?

"She has been having nightmares," Callie stated the obvious. "I will just wait for you outside the door to give you a few minutes of privacy. I dare not go further or your mother will see me sent to Berwyck's dungeon for disobeying her."

Calliope left the room but left the door slightly ajar. Gwendolyn supposed she was lucky to have even just a few minutes alone with Neville. Still… she wondered if perhaps she was still sleeping and only dreamed he was here.

"Gwendolyn, my love." Neville's voice could not have been sweeter than an angel sent from the heavens above to forgive her sins. Warm hands reached for her cold ones and brought her fingertips to his lips. It was really him! And surely he was her angel, and seeing him again meant she had been forgiven whilst on earth.

"Neville?" Her voice sounded as shaky as she felt.

"I have you, my love," he said. Sitting down next to her on the bed, he took hold of her and brought her into his embrace. "I will never let you go again."

She buried her head into his chest and began crying in earnest. He held true to his word and continued to hold her whilst she cried. She began mumbling incoherently about the ordeals she had faced in her dreams. Heaven. Hell.

Bernard claiming to have power over her for all time along with every inch of fear that the man she loved would not wait for her. All the worries that had consumed her during the months that had separated them came pouring out. She never thought to feel again the security Neville's arms brought her. How wrong she had been to doubt what had been between them from the very beginning.

Neville pressed a kiss to her forehead. "Shush. You are speaking nonsense now. How you thought I would not wait for you is beyond my understanding. You are the very air I breathe, my dearest love. I am only a shadow of a man without you by my side. We have only had a brief respite from one another. I have just now attested to your own dear mother that I love you. I am afraid you are stuck with me… that is if you would care to spend the rest of our lives together."

Gwendolyn took a moment to compose herself before she at last looked into the hazel eyes of the man she adored. She reached up to touch his cheek. "You really are here?"

"I would not want to be anywhere else than by your side, Gwen."

"But what about the rest of my time in mourning? I would hate for Society and your own family to think unkindly of me… or you," she whispered.

"My family will adore you as much as I do. Besides, I believe my younger brother is already looking forward to having you in our family. He took quite a liking to you in the brief encounter you had with him."

Gwendolyn blushed when she remembered barging into Neville's home. "What he must think of me," she muttered.

"I assure you he thought you most daring to show up as you did, never fear. But you have not answered me, sweet

Gwendolyn."

She looked up into the eyes of the man who had stolen her heart months ago. Her thoughts were so jumbled with embarrassment she could not remember what he had asked her. "You will need to ask again because I am afraid our conversation has gotten away from me."

Gwendolyn watched in fascination when the love of her life released her, only to drop to one knee upon the floor. Reaching into his jacket, he pulled out a ring. The diamond sparkled much like her eyes must surely be shining.

"Gwendolyn Marie Worthington Sandhurst, please do me the honor of taking me as your husband. I promise I shall spend all of my days showering you with all the love my heart holds for you and even after my last dying breath, I will continue to love only you."

"Oh, Neville," she cried out in happiness.

"Is that a yes?" he asked appearing as though he was holding his breath whilst he awaited her answer.

"Yes! A thousand times and more, yes!"

Neville slipped the ring onto her finger. She barely had time to catch a glimpse of it before he sealed their promises to one another with a kiss. It could not have happened soon enough, for their last bit of privacy was about to be interrupted when Callie quickly opened the door wide and took her place near the hearth. Her voice coming closer as she spoke, her mother was calling out their names.

EPILOGUE

$\mathcal{G}$ WENDOLYN'S SMILE SURELY nearly split her face as she stared at the handsome gentleman before her.

"You may kiss your bride, Lord Drayton," the clergyman proclaimed, after finishing his blessing upon the couple before him.

"Finally," Neville whispered, before leaning forward to seal their marriage with their first kiss as husband and wife.

Gwendolyn swore she heard a collective sigh from those in the congregation and nearest to the altar. Turning to face their guests, she took her bouquet of flowers from Callie and began to proceed down the aisle of the church. Their wedding had been perfect; a day that dreams were made of. This ceremony was so very different from her first that Gwendolyn was afraid to blink in fear she would wake up from her sleep.

Her mother's and brothers' faces said more than any words could express and even Neville's parents appeared happy for them, despite that they had waited no longer than the required amount of time to wed. His brother winked as she walked by and Gwendolyn held back her own laughter.

The door to their carriage opened and Neville helped her inside. She quickly arranged the length of her dress so the door did not shut upon its train. Neville squeezed himself into the seat next to her and the carriage was set into motion.

"Happy? Or are you already regretting marrying me?" he quietly asked.

She raised a brow in his direction, suppressing her amusement. She knew him well enough now that she could sense when he was jesting with her. "Really, Drayton? These are the first words you are going to speak to me after just now making me your wife?"

He leaned forward to nuzzle her ear causing her to shiver in anticipation of what the night would bring. "I do so adore it when you are upset with me. Those eyes of yours sparkle like the brightest of jewels."

Gwendolyn tried, she really did, to remain looking cross at him but how could she. Their laughter broke out in unison and she leaned forward to kiss her husband. "We have a lot of time to make up for. It is too bad that we have a whole wedding dinner to get through and I will not even begin to think about how long the dancing will go on for."

"Hartford seems as though he is doing his best to make amends for his part in your earlier marriage."

She quickly placed her fingers over his lips, which he began kissing. "Today, we will not speak of our past and only look forward to a bright new future."

"I love you, Gwendolyn. For all of time, my soul will belong only to you."

"My darling husband, you have no idea how long I have

waited to hear you say those words to me. I love you as well."

Hours later whilst Gwendolyn lay next to her slumbering husband, she gave a silent prayer of thanks. She had much to be grateful for, which certainly included the man to whom she was snuggled. She had no idea what their future would bring, but she knew she and Neville would face life together. She closed her eyes with a contented sigh. She had found love with the man of her dreams, and safely married they now had nothing but time. She could not ask for more…

Bonus Material

Dear Reader:

I hope you enjoyed Gwendolyn and Neville's journey to finding love in my new series, *A Family of Worth*. This has been a long time in the making. *Nothing But Time* is actually a prequel to the very first story I ever wrote entitled *One Moment in Time* and will feature Gwendolyn's brother Edmond as the hero. I'll be working on the final edits and hope to publish this soon.

I also hope you like the extra twist I put in this story by connecting my *Knights of Berwyck* series by having the Worthington's related (several generations removed, of course) to Amiria and Dristan from *If My Heart Could See You*. I just couldn't resist connecting the families.

The following pages are short stories that appeared in the Bluestocking Belles' Teatime Tattler blog. I hope you enjoy these extra insights in the further development of my characters from *Nothing But Time*.

No letter to my readers would be complete if I did not express my gratitude to you for all your support. You've joined my street team, shared my posts on social media, gave my books glowing reviews causing this author to do a happy dance, and have contacted me to let me know how much you've enjoyed my novels. I am humbly grateful to each and every one of you. I have more stories coming soon for your reading pleasure. Thank you again for all you do on my behalf. Your efforts do not go unnoticed.

Until the next time, I look forward to seeing your posts on social media.

With warm regards,

Sherry Ewing

Rumors abound in London once more

Edmond Worthington, 9th Duke of Hartford looked up in annoyance when his study door slammed opened, the paintings on the walls trembling from the force. He had wondered how long it would take his younger brother to find him once he was told the news.

"How could you, Hartford?" Brandon shouted. He quickly made his way across the room and displayed his frustration by pounding his fists upon the desk. "Tell me it is not true."

Edmond's brow rose in understanding; not that this would in some way change the situation. "Mother told you?"

"I have not spoken to mother as yet. I read about it in some disgusting gossip rag. Dammit Hartford, how can you be so callous?" Brandon fumed before stepping back while he awaited an answer. His face turned red with anger while his hands balled into fists at his side.

Edmond nodded his head towards the sideboard. "Make it two."

Brandon once more crossed the room to take hold of two crystal glasses before surveying his choice of liquor. He grabbed the whiskey. "Perhaps I should bring the bottle." Setting the glasses down, he began pouring, not bothering to be neat about it.

Edmond quickly moved his correspondence to save it from a good drenching. He motioned for Brandon to take a seat. Reaching for his glass he took a long hard pull of the fiery whiskey. This discussion was nothing to celebrate, although his sister's impending marriage should have been.

"How can you honor such a contract between

Gwendolyn and someone old enough to be her father? Sandhurst is hardly what I would call a young woman's ideal of a loving husband," Brandon said. He proceeded to down his drink and then refilled it.

Edmond sighed. "Yes, well, I have to agree with you on that but my hands are tied. Father begged me on his death bed to honor their contract. Why he made such an arrangement with the man I cannot say."

"Blackmail, perhaps?"

Edmond shrugged. "I have no idea, but whatever our father got himself into, he made a bargain with the very devil. I am honor bound to see the matter done. If father had not passed on requiring us to observe our year of mourning, Gwendolyn would already have been wed. She did agree to the marriage, if you will recall."

"At least it will not be on my conscious that I made her marry Sandhurst."

Edmond rubbed his neck. "I do not look forward to the confrontation. Her tears will most likely be my downfall."

"At least you were not in attendance at a bookshop when I went to purchase a novel for mother. To hear our lovely sister's name bandied about while those *ladies* were sniggering behind their fans at such news was almost more than I could bear," Brandon said with a grimace. He pulled the newspaper from his jacket and tossed it across the desk. "At least it is not on the front but buried on the seventh page."

"*The Teatime Tattler*? I have not heard of it," Edmond said reaching for the paper, "not that I have the time or the inclination to read about what the gossipmongers have to say."

"It is all the rage with society. Normally such filth does

not interest me either, but I heard Gwendolyn's name mentioned so it perked my interest. You will not be pleased."

Edmond turned to the page Brandon had indicated and read:

> *It appears, dear reader, that an impending marriage will shortly be announced between none other than Lady Gwendolyn Worthington and the elderly Lord Bernard Sandhurst. With news of the haste in their nuptials, will the bride and groom be making another announcement shortly thereafter of cause to celebrate again not nine months hence?*

Edmond balled up the newspaper. How dare someone assume that Gwendolyn was pregnant of all things? He finished his drink, disgusted with society and with himself for having to honor his father's decree.

A Reluctant Bride

Gwendolyn flinched at the priest's words.

"You may kiss the bride, Lord Sandhurst," he repeated since she had not paid the least bit of attention whilst he sealed her fate to her groom. As if she needed a reminder that she was now wed to a gentleman not of her choosing.

She raised her red puffy eyes and stared at the man who was so old that he surely had one foot perched on the edge of his grave. How her father could promise her to a man of his ilk was beyond her imagination. That her own brother would honor the contract after their sire's passing and condemn her to a loveless marriage tore at her heart. And the pressure he had put on her to give her consent! She would never forgive Hartford for as long as she drew breath in her body.

"My dear wife," Sandhurst murmured with an appreciative glare. His eyes traveled the length of her body. He did not even give her the courtesy of abstaining from such a leer whilst still in a church and not behind closed doors.

The priest cleared his throat and gave Gwendolyn his own condemning look that she should be responding to her husband.

She said nothing; she simply looked at the floor showing her disdain at the union. She trembled when she glanced up and saw him lick his lips as though he were about to devour a tasty treat. He leaned forward. She choked back her anger.

It took every inch of strength not to allow her husband to see how much he repulsed her. His mouth hovered over her own before his head plunged ever downward to capture her lips. Inwardly, she groaned. His kiss was so much worse than she could have ever imagined, and when his hand clamped around her waist bringer her closer, she swore she was going to retch. Right here. In a holy chapel. God help her.

She pulled away so abruptly she lost her balance and would have spilled backwards if it were not for his firm hold continuing to keep her close... as close as could be expected, that is, given his girth. She shuddered. Lord Bernard Sandhurst chuckled in amusement. Gwendolyn could not find anything in this situation that would be cause for his merriment, but he was certainly pleased considering the gleam she saw in his pale cold eyes.

Sandhurst took her elbow and began escorting her down the aisle of the church that was relatively empty. As empty as her heart. Her husband nodded to several acquaintances. Gwendolyn passed her mother who hid a handkerchief that she surely had used to dry her eyes. Her brother, Brandon, looked as grim as she herself felt. She would not acknowledge Hartford's presence. He may hold their father's title of duke but as far as she was concerned, he was dead to her. As dead as her emotions would become if she was going to survive this marriage.

As they reached the rear of the church, she stumbled once more. There, barely hidden in the last pew, was a man scribbling away with his quill. Oh no, she thought. Please do not let him be from the Teatime Tattler. But luck was not on her side this day. God surely must have forsaken her for the marriage had gone through and the reporter could not have been more pleased with the day's outcome. Mr. Clemens raised his eyes when she drew near and had the unmitigated nerve to salute her with his ever-efficient quill.

As Gwendolyn was helped into the carriage, she knew it

would not be long before all of London read about her recent marriage. She could already hear the sniggering of the gossipmongers as they laughed about the duke's daughter who could not find a man to marry who was near her own age. She would be the laughing stock of society by the Tattler's morning edition.

The carriage door slammed shut as Gwendolyn took her seat, much like the reality that her former life was now over. She could already feel the ice quickly surrounding her heart knowing she would never find love as Lord Bernard Sandhurst's wife. Only a miracle could save her from her fate and believing in miracles was for fools...

A not so casual stroll in the park

Mrs. Cassandra Vaughn adjusted her wrap about her shoulders and peered ahead on the path of the tree-lined park. Was it only just yesterday that her lover, Neville Quinn, Earl of Drayton, had ended their association? It seemed he had wasted no time and was in a hurry to find her replacement. She watched the couple ahead of her continue their casual stroll. If her eyes did not mistake her, Cassandra's rival for Drayton's attention was none other than Lady Gwendolyn Sandhurst, sister to the Duke of Hartford and his younger brother Lord Brandon Worthington. Drayton would be treading dangerous waters if he were to trifle with a married woman. If the woman's husband did not call him out, her brothers certainly would!

"Why are we walking when there is a perfectly fine carriage waiting for us to ride in?" Mrs. Patience Moore complained bitterly.

Cassandra strained her neck to peer at the bend in the trail up ahead, wishing the trees out of her line of sight so she could see what Drayton was up to. Another tug on her sleeve brought her attention back to her companion. Patience Moore had no patience whatsoever, but had been a dear friend when she had most needed one after she lost her husband. That they were both on the lookout for their next benefactor was reason enough for a walk in the park where they could check out any new prospects. A widow down on her luck sometimes resorted to unpleasant and difficult situations beyond those she had been raised to.

"I needed to stretch my legs. The walk will do us good," Cassandra finally answered but sighed in frustration when Patience went to a nearby tree to remove a pebble from her shoe. Now she had lost sight of the man. She must be losing her mind. Why in the world was she following him in the first place?

"Honestly, Cassandra, I did not mean for my feet to suffer such abuse today. These shoes were not made for traipsing about in the woods, dear." Patience adjusted her bonnet, linked her arm through Cassandra's, and urged her onward. "If we must continue, let us be quick about it so we can get back to your driver and enjoy our outing from the comfort of a padded seat."

As they rounded the bend that had obstructed her view of Drayton's whereabouts, Cassandra skidded to a very unladylike halt and pushed Patience behind a tree. Her eyes narrowed with jealousy, although why such an emotion seemed to be plaguing her she could not say. They had made no commitment to one another nor expressed words of love. Their relationship had been a convenience for them both. Why, then, did Cassandra's heart feel as though it were being stabbed with a knife when she observed Drayton carrying Lady Sandhurst in his arms before depositing her on a park bench?

"Is that not?" Patience began.

"Yes."

"Are you not still with him?"

"Not as of yesterday." Cassandra's reply was so quiet the sound was almost lost on the wind. "I have seen enough. Shall we return to the carriage?" She could not keep herself from one last glance at Neville. She should have refrained, since her heart lurched yet again when he once more picked up the lady.

Not caring whether or not Patience followed her, Cassandra hastily cut through the trees to reach the main walkway of the park. Looking for her driver, she saw none other than Lord Brandon Worthington driving his own rig, as if she conjured him up. He slowed the team of horses as he came nearer and gave her a brilliant smile. An encouraging sign if Cassandra ever saw one. Perhaps the day had not been such a waste after all. He had just pulled the carriage to a halt and tipped his hat when she heard Lord Brandon's name being called. With a hasty apology, he flicked the reins and Cassandra watched as Drayton deposited the gentleman's sister inside the rig. They were gone before she had even had a chance to catch her breath.

She was occupied with thoughts of Lord Brandon being the next handsome gentleman to warm her bed, when her driver came abreast of them. After accepting assistance from her footman, she rearranged her dress and she relaxed in her carriage. As the team began to move, she groaned aloud. There on the walk was none other than Samuel Clemmons, editor of that nasty *Teatime Tattler* gossip rag, scribbling away on a note pad. She wondered for the remainder of the night what page she would find her name upon come the following day.

Someone Always Sees

Lady Constance Whittles made her way across the crowded ballroom after finishing a lively dance with none other than the dashing Lord Digby Osgood. She had taken delight with the free time allotted her since she no longer worked at the bookshop. She was more than pleased with any opportunity to get to know the gentleman further. She might as well take advantage of every moment she could spend in his company before she began her new position at Miss Clemens's Oxford Street Book Palace & Tea Rooms.

Digby led her over to a chair near a window where a slight breeze blew in through the open balcony doors. "Wine or punch?" he asked once she was seated.

"Punch would be divine," she said with a parched throat.

"I will be right back. Do you mind if I have a brief conversation with Frederick before I return? I see he just arrived with Margaret?"

"By all means, go right ahead. I shall be fine here watching the dancing until your return."

He gave a brief bow and disappeared through the crowded room while Constance snapped open her fan to bring relief to her flushed face. She was not sitting alone long before she heard the quiet whisperings of two women behind her in the darkened entryway. She did not mean to overhear their conversations but they made no attempt to quiet their voices. Most likely they thought the music would dim their gossiping from traveling any further than between them.

"How could you not have heard such distressing news, Abigail?"

A loud sigh was heard. "Good heavens, Prudence. You

have the latest *news* on any given hour of the day. How am I supposed to keep up with you on whatever bit of gossip that is none of my business in the first place?"

With a discrete glance behind her, Constance held back the urge to roll her eyes. The Danver sisters... She had met them on several occasions in the bookshop. They were relatively harmless creatures, yet the elder of the two had a penchant for wanting to share whatever tidbit was been bandied about without much thought. Thankfully her younger sibling kept her in check.

"This is not gossip but fact and is regarding the son of our hosts," Prudence continued.

"Lord Drayton?"

"His brother is far too young to be of much interest… yet. Of course this is about none other than Neville Quinn." The sound of a small slap was heard. "What was that for? You hurt my arm."

"You are over exaggerating, I barely touched you. Besides, beware you are not overheard addressing him so informally lest you wish to be the next one people are talking about," Abigale scolded.

"Pish, posh! I think not. Besides, I would not dare let my reputation be ruined because I was having an affair."

"Whatever are you talking about, Prudence?

"Honestly, Abigail, do you know nothing of what is going on around you?"

"Apparently not, but I have the distinct feeling you shall fill me in."

"Lord Drayton is having an affair with a married woman."

Laughter came from the younger sister. "Is that all? Look inside, sister. Half the men in that room are probably having an affair or have taken a mistress."

"But Abigail, do you not wish to hear with whom he—"

"No, not really," Abigail stated. "Let us return to the ball. I am sure we can find something more interesting to converse about."

"No husband of mine would ever dare have an affair on me," Prudence muttered.

"If my husband attempted such, I would see him gelded. He would not be much use to anyone after such a fate," Abigale added with a laugh.

The two women moved on leaving Constance to ponder their words, not that she would be one to spread their tale further. She noticed when Lord Drayton entered the room with two other gentlemen Constance was unfamiliar with. He looked on edge as though he took no pleasure at being in attendance at his parent's event. He gave a meager smile towards his mother before moving from Constance's view.

Lord Digby returned with her punch and after a few sips, they moved onto the dance floor. The Danver sister's conversation still lingered in her mind causing Constance to wonder the fate of the poor woman who must have stolen Lord Drayton's heart.

OTHER BOOKS BY SHERRY EWING

If My Heart Could See You

When you're enemies, does love have a fighting chance? Amiria of Berwyck vows to protect her people by pledging her oath of fealty to the very enemy who has laid siege to her home. Dristan, the Devil's Dragon of Blackmore, has a reputation to uphold as champion knight of his king. Lies, treachery, and deceit attempt to tear them apart, but only love will bring them together

For All of Ever: The Knights of Berwyck, A Quest Through Time Novel (Book One)

Sometimes to find your future, you must look to the past... Katherine dreamed of her knight all her life yet how could she know she'd be thrown back into the past? Nothing prepares Riorden for the beautiful vision of a strangely clad ghost appearing in his chamber. Centuries keep them apart but will Time give them a chance at finding love?

Only For You: The Knights of Berwyck, A Quest Through Time Novel (Book Two)

Sometimes it's hard to remember that true love conquers all, only after the battle is over... Katherine has it all but settling into her duties at Warkworth is dangerous to her well-being. Consumed with memories of his father, Riorden must deal with his sire's widow. Torn apart, Time becomes their enemy while Marguerite continues her ploy to keep Riorden at her side. With all hope lost, will Katherine & Riorden find a way to save their marriage?

A Knight To Call My Own

When your heart is broken, is love still worth the risk? Lynet of Clan MacLaren knows how it feels to love someone and not have that love returned. Ian MacGillivray has returned to Berwyck in search of a bride. Who will claim the fair Lynet? The price will be high to ensure her safety and even higher to win her love.

To Follow My Heart: The Knights of Berwyck, A Quest Through Time Novel (Book Three)

Love is a leap. Sometimes you need to jump… Jenna Sinclair is dealing with a horrendous break up with her fiancé when she finds herself pulled through time to twelfth century England. Fletcher Monroe has spent too much time pining away for a woman who will never be his until a strangely clad woman magically appears. Torn between the past and the present, will their growing love survive a journey through Time?

Hearts Across Time: The Knights of Berwyck (Books One & Two)

Sometimes all you need is to just believe… Hearts Across Time is a special edition box set that combines Katherine and Riorden's stories together from For All of Ever and Only For You.

Under the Mistletoe

A new suitor seeks her hand. An old flame holds her heart. Which one will she meet under the kissing bough? When Margaret Templeton is requested to act as hostess at a Christmas party she did not think she would see the man who once held her heart. Frederick Maddock, Viscount Beacham never forgot the young woman he had fallen in love with. Will the two finally put down their differences and once again fall in love?

A Kiss For Charity

Young widow, Grace, Lady de Courtenay, has no idea how a close encounter with a rake at a masquerade ball would make her yearn for love again. Lord Nicholas Lacey is captivated by a lovely young woman he encounters at a masquerade. Considering the company she keeps, she might be interested in becoming his mistress. From the darkened paths of Vauxhall Gardens to a countryside estate called Hollystone Hall, Nicholas and Grace must set aside their differences in order to let love into their hearts.

You can find out more about Sherry's work on her website at www.SherryEwing.com and at online retailers.

COMING SOON

Love Will Find You
The Knights of Berwyck

SOCIAL MEDIA

Website: www.SherryEwing.com
Bluestocking Belles: www.bluestockingbelles.net/
Hearts Through Time: www.heartsthroughtime.com
Bookbub: www.bookbub.com/authors/sherry-ewing
Facebook: www.Facebook.com/SherryEwingAuthor
Goodreads:
www.Goodreads.com/author/show/8382315.Sherry_Ewi
ng
Pinterest: www.Pinterest.com/SherryLEwing
Twitter: www.Twitter.com/Sherry_Ewing

Sign Me Up!

Newsletter: www.eepurl.com/-jGfj
Facebook Street Team:
www.facebook.com/groups/799623313455472/

Email: Sherry@SherryEwing.com

ABOUT THE AUTHOR

Sherry Ewing picked up her first historical romance when she was a teenager and has been hooked ever since. A bestselling author, she writes historical & time travel romances to awaken the soul one heart at a time. Always wanting to write a novel but busy raising her children, she finally took the plunge in 2008 and wrote her first Regency. She is a member of Romance Writers of America, the Beau Monde & the Bluestocking Belles. Sherry is currently working on her next novel and when not writing, she can be found in the San Francisco area at her day job as an Information Technology Specialist. You can learn more about Sherry and her published work at www.SherryEwing.com.